THE UNDYING

NAMELESS - BOOK FOUR

NIKKI ROBB

THE UNDYING

NAMELESS - BOOK FOUR

NIKKI ROBB

ISBN: Paperback: 978-1-964036-09-0
ISBN: Hardback: 978-1-964036-22-9

This novel is a work of fiction, any similarities to real people and events are entirely coincidental.

Cover Design by Nikki Robb
Interior Design by Rachel McEwan
Printed and distributed by Kindle Direct Publishing

First Printing Edition

CONTENT WARNINGS

This novel includes and alludes to things that may be concerning, such as murder, vampires, blood drinking, graphic sex, sexual assault, rape, cancer, descriptions of torture, death of a parent and family member, victim-blaming, panic attacks, brief thoughts of self-harm, PTSD, discrimination, hate crimes, parental neglect, and harassment.

Please consider these before continuing.

To everyone who believes immortality is best enjoyed
with a healthy dose of supernatural drama and a whole lot
of fanged affection.

ORPHEUS

PROLOGUE

"You're the only one who can keep us from death, Orpheus." The common phrase my mother spoke echoed as I opened my eyes. As they adjusted to the sight around them, I couldn't help but notice that my throat felt raw and pained. The fresh scent of open air assaulted my nostrils. Before me, the Bugeac Plains stretched in every direction, broken by numerous ravines and gullies that sliced through the expanse like veins beneath the skin. Panic consumed me. My heart should have been pounding in my chest from the disorientation, but I noticed with a jolt that it was unnaturally still.

My chest rose and fell as I hyperventilated, feeling the fear grip my unbeating heart as I attempted to piece together the puzzle that led me to this very moment.

I had traveled to Moldova on the trade route with my family's stockpile of grain and livestock to sell at the market. Panicked, I glanced around, looking for any sign of my cart, my animals, or any money received from their sale. When I found nothing, I felt a sinking feeling in the pit of my stomach. Despite the strange fog that hung over the memory of the last several hours, I knew that my family would unlikely survive the coming winter without that money. My mother was counting on me to provide for her and my sister. If I couldn't do that, I was useless.

I was the only thing standing between them and death's doorway.

They'd told me that. They relied on me. And I had failed them.

I stood and began stumbling through the open plains, desperate for a clue of why I was in the middle of nowhere, covered in blood, left with nothing but the clothes on my back. My body felt disjointed, like there was something almost new about it. The morning air's chill caressed my skin, yet I felt no cold. I took tentative steps across the plains, noticing an unfamiliar strength in my limbs. Every sensation was unbelievably heightened. I could feel the texture of each blade of grass beneath my fingers and hear the distant rustle of leaves miles away. My senses had sharpened to an almost painful clarity. The world around me seemed more vibrant and alive, yet I felt detached as if observing it through a veil.

Then, I caught a scent— sweet, warm, and utterly intoxicating. It was unlike anything I had ever smelled, stirring something primal and animalistic within me. I turned, nearly involuntarily, following the scent with instinctual precision. My legs moved with a fluidity and speed that would have shocked me if I had been in the state of mind to analyze it and carried me swiftly across the plain.

In the distance, I saw a traveler, a solitary figure making his way through the wilderness. An almost calm sense of adventure and excitement rippled off of him. I felt a shift within me as I approached, a primal and wicked hunger awakening. My vision seemed to tunnel as I focused solely on the stranger's pulse, faint but steady. My mouth watered, and my fangs, which I hadn't realized I possessed, descended with a sharp ache.

My thoughts returned to the night before, still hazy but slowly coming into focus. I arrived in town late and decided to commemorate the end of my long journey with an ale at the pub. The firelight flickered warmly in the cozy tavern, casting long shadows that danced on the walls as the patrons enjoyed the company of others and the taste of their drinks.

A man, a stranger, commanded the room with his presence and caught my undying attention nearly immediately. He spun animated tales of the unnatural and the demonic. His voice was a deep, velvety baritone that seemed to weave a spell over everyone who listened. He whispered stories of terrible creatures of the night. Of long, sharp fangs. Of blood-thirsty hunters. He argued the validity of his stories with other patrons who were well into their cups. He warned us of the dangers of trusting the monsters of the night.

I recalled how his eyes had lingered on me, an unsettling intensity in his gaze. I remembered the shiver that had run down my spine, a threatening warning I had dismissed as mere theatrics.

As the night wore on, the stranger made his way to my table, seemingly emboldened by how intently I was interested in his tales. He offered to buy me a drink, and I accepted, honestly curious about this enigmatic storyteller and how he became so interested in such tales. We talked long into the night, his stories slowly becoming darker and more vivid. He had produced a flask at one point, insisting I try a sip of what he claimed was a rare wine. The thick, coppery liquid had burned as it went down, and my vision had blurred almost immediately.

Despite my best efforts to recall, that's where most of my memory ends. I had left the pub with him, my steps unsteady, my senses dulled. Whatever liquid he had given me was acidic on my tongue as he led me out of town into the vast openness of the plains, speaking in low, hypnotic tones. There, under the moonlight, he revealed his true nature, his eyes glowing with an unnatural light, his fangs gleaming as he bit into my neck.

The change that had occurred within me was undeniable now. Somehow, I had been transformed into something of nightmares, a creature from the stories I'd only ever dismissed as fiction. The new, animalistic side of my mind begged me to sink my new fangs into the neck of the traveler before me and drain the blood within their veins, yet a part of my human mind desperately clung to the last vestiges of rationality.

The traveler continued on the path, unaware of the predator that had awakened in his midst. As the first rays of sunlight crept over the horizon, I felt the biting sting against my skin. A burning sensation crawled across the pale canvas of my skin. Quickly, I turned away from the traveler and his tempting blood, retreating to the shadows, searching for refuge from the assaulting sun and the world that was forever changed. I'd have to learn to survive in this new version of my existence, and someday, I'd need to embrace the darkness that was now my home.

It took several weeks of traveling only under the safety of the moonlight, but when I arrived at my home, I saw the effects of my failure firsthand. I found them too late. The scene seared itself into my mind, my mother and sister lying lifeless on the cold, hard ground. Their faces were gaunt, their eyes hollow. I had ventured, unwillingly, into the land of the dead, and due to my carelessness, my family had followed swiftly behind.

I fell to my knees before my mother's frail and lifeless body. Her hands folded across her chest as if she had been praying. Praying for me to return, to do what I swore I would, and to protect them. I learned then that even though my heart did not beat, it could still break.

My mother's words whispered to me in a moment of rare tenderness, returned to my mind. "You're the only one who can keep us from death, Orpheus." Those words echoed in my mind, now a cruel reminder of my inability to protect them.

Tears blurred my vision as I reached out to touch my sister's cold hand, the realization hitting me with brutal clarity. I had failed them, but should the occasion arise, I wouldn't fail again.

I clenched my fists, feeling a surge of determination rise within me. This pain, this loss, would not be in vain. I vowed then and there, as I knelt beside the lifeless bodies of the ones I loved most that I would never let this happen again. If I ever let myself care for another person again, I would protect them with a fierceness that knew no bounds.

"I'm sorry, I'm so sorry, I couldn't keep you from death," I whispered, my voice trembling with resolve. "I swear to you, I'll never make this mistake again. If I ever open my heart to another, I will protect them so fiercely that death itself will tremble at my presence. I will not only stand in the way of death's door, but I will burn it down."

The vow took root deep within me, a burning promise that would shape my every action from that moment forward. No one I loved would ever suffer because of my failure again. I would be their shield, their guardian, their protector. And I would ensure that the darkness that had claimed my family would never touch those I loved.

ATHENA

ONE

My heightened senses were going to take some getting used to. In fact, it all was. Everything about me had shifted in a way that felt so foreign, yet somehow still comfortable. Although, maybe I shouldn't classify the burning in my throat and the overwhelming desire to drain the blood of any living creature near me as 'comfortable.' Familiar, maybe. Which is a wild thought. How could something so unnatural feel familiar? But it did. So, when the first gust of the ocean breeze hit my nostrils, assaulting me with the scent of saltwater, cool air, and comfort, I knew we were almost home. The trip took longer than it should have, but I was forced to travel under cover of night. Orpheus promised that once we eliminated the immediate threat to our lives, we would travel to New Orleans to visit the vampire who gave them the ability to walk in the sunlight. I was already desperate for that day, feeling useless during the daylight hours when the others would be scouting ahead, gathering supplies, or making moves toward accomplishing our goal, all while I hid out in a cave or an abandoned factory, confined to the shadowed corners like a monster.

I felt like humanity was slipping away from me the longer I remained in the dark, but still, I clung to what made me *me*. I'd need that anchor if I were going to survive this.

"What are we going to do about the police? I've been missing for over two weeks. And Greg? What if they ask about Greg?" I asked softly as we slowed our run to a much more comfortable walking pace. Archer slid off Silas' back, grumbling about how 'he wouldn't need to piggyback if we had just rented a car.' Orpheus turned to face me and placed a gentle hand on my cheek. His previously chilled touch felt almost warm against my newly frozen skin.

"We tell them as much of the truth as they need to know, then fill in the blanks. Greg attacked you in your shop, and when you got away, you knew you needed to get out of town in case he tried again. You left with your new partners to get some distance and make sure it was safe for you to return and file a report against him." He caressed my face as he formulated the plan.

"And when they ask why I didn't call them?" I prompt.

His eyebrows furrowed, twisting his stoic face into a more pained look, and he nodded once. "If you feel comfortable, you can cite the lack of assistance this particular station offered during your last report of violence from a male figure."

I sucked in a breath as the memory of the cold dingy room and the detective's even colder judgment returned to me.

"You don't have to say a damn thing if you don't want to," Silas chimed in, his overprotective urges surging to the surface. I ran a finger along the serpents that ran along my clavicle and felt our bond pulse with warmth. He sighed and nodded, a soft smile playing on his lips.

"Am I missing something important?" Archer asked, glancing between us, no doubt sensing my hesitance.

"You've missed a lot, Archer," I replied softly, not with malice but rather with pain. We had missed each other's entire lives because of our father's selfishness. He nodded, content to leave it there for now, but I knew we needed to set aside time to truly get to know each other when things were safer.

Samara came up behind me, laying a hand on my shoulder before addressing the group. "We should head straight to the police department. Then we can go see your grandma," she said softly.

"And Davia," Archer replied. When I turned my eyes questioningly toward him, he shrugged. "She called me while you were at Nameless. She is worried about you." The blush on his face told me there was a little more to the story than that, but I didn't care right now. I needed to get through the next few hours so I could see the people I loved. The conversation I needed to have with my grandma felt like a heavy weight on my chest, but I knew it needed to happen. Maybe I'd see Davia first. I knew that was like prolonging the inevitable, but a furious little piece of my heart that felt betrayed by my grandmother wasn't ready to face her and listen to her explain why she kept so much from me.

We stepped out from behind the canopy of trees and wilderness to see the quaint town of Shockgrove. It was early evening, just an hour after the sun had set. The faint remnants of the day cast a pale orange glow along the water. Sparkling lights dotted the streets and the pier, sparkling with warmth. I'd spent so much of my life wishing for a way out of this tiny little town and the painful memories that seem so intrinsically tied to it. But in this light, from this angle, knowing all I know now…I can finally see this place for what it is. Home.

My eye caught on the faded lighthouse standing sentinel, overlooking the quiet hamlet. My dead heart ached as I recalled the memories I held there with my mother and how, too soon, they would start to disappear, falling victim to this new existence.

Orpheus, understanding my pain or perhaps feeling it for himself, squeezed his arm around my waist. Laz leaned into me on the other side, kissing gently against my temple. I released a soft sigh, then stepped forward, preparing to face the aftermath of what we had left behind.

*

Three hours later, after the police had thoroughly and relentlessly investigated my story and extensively questioned each of us, save Archer, who had gone ahead to my house, we were allowed to leave the station. The moon hung in the star-dotted sky, and all remnants of daylight had sufficiently been replaced by the inky darkness of night.

The police, albeit suspicious about some parts of my story, seemed to buy the tale we had weaved completely. I think we were lucky that Detective Barnes was the one who was assigned to lead my case and not her less-than-sensitive partner, Detective Argent. Apparently, there was a security camera on the front of a business just down the pier that caught footage of me, bloodied and battered, scampering down the pier away from The Maine Plotline, followed closely by an angry and feral-looking Gregory. I couldn't shake the involuntary chill that ran down my spine as I watched that footage. The camera, thankfully, did not have the right angle to catch the moment we fought on the pier. So, the police seemed to accept that I got away, found my partners, and got the hell out of town.

The police told us that they had begun to piece together evidence left from the rental house where The Wanderers had been staying. They claimed their running theory was that Greg broke into the house where I was seen after we skipped town, hoping he could find me there.

Detective Barnes assured me she would do everything possible to keep me safe from Greg, and I thanked her. The gratitude felt like ash on my tongue, though. How was it that they believed me now? After everything, all it took was fifteen seconds of blurry footage to prove the truth. But when my shaking, fragile form sat in that room all those years ago, they couldn't be bothered to grant me an ounce of sympathy.

My cold heart ached, and I wanted to cry for the version of me who had to suffer at this department's arrogant and dismissive hands when it truly mattered.

Detective Barnes told me to stay in town. I promised I would unless I felt Greg was going to hurt me again. She urged me to call the station if that were the case instead of running but seemed to recognize the fear in my eyes. A fear I didn't have to fake because while I knew that he went over the railing, I had no way of knowing if he survived the drop and if he was, in fact, lying in wait until his chance came again. Barnes saw that terror reflected in me, and I could tell her leniency was in response to that. A woman understands that fear more than a man ever could.

Now, the five of us stood alone in the Shockgrove Police Station parking lot, a soft moon casting a cool light across our tired faces, but a small weight was lifted. It was just one of many crushing pounds of problems to deal with, but anything that made our load easier to carry was worth it.

"Do you want to go see your grandma? I can go get Archer?" Silas said. I smiled softly. Despite their…shaky introduction, my mate and brother seemed to have formed a bond. Hell, maybe it was the piggyback.

Or it could be the fact that Silas jumped back into the Hunter's den to save Archer from the vicious hands of his father after he risked everything to help us escape.

Probably the piggyback.

"No," I replied quietly. "I'm not ready to hear the answers she has." Silas nodded.

"Do you want to go home?"

Did I? Yes, eventually. But there was someplace I needed to go first.

"I need to see Davia."

Orpheus and Laz agreed to walk me to her house while the others returned to my house to "sunproof it." I tried not to be saddened by the thought of my normally warm and cozy home feeling like a cave when I returned and focused instead on the task ahead of me. Was I going to tell her the truth? Should I? Would that put her at risk in the eyes of Nameless? Would she even believe me? What if she smells too good, and I shift right in front of her? Should I drink before I go in there? Panic was bubbling up in my chest as we walked, and I knew Orpheus could feel it, but he had thankfully not drawn attention to it.

Laz's hand in mine and Orpheus' calming presence at my back was a gentle grounding, reminding me where and who I was. Despite the changes I'd undergone, I was and will always be who I always have been.

"Tell her whatever you need to, Athena. Whatever you'd like to. This secret is yours too now. Yours to share, or yours to keep," Laz offered as they turned toward Davia's home. I didn't even bother asking how they knew exactly where her house was. They had probably been watching out for me during my little staycation while I wrestled with the existence of the supernatural. Something that probably would have freaked me out back then, but now was something I understood all too well now that the mate bond thrummed so loudly in my chest.

"Thank you," I whispered in response as we stopped at the end of her driveway.

"She's going to be glad that you're ok, first and foremost," Laz said softly.

"You should drink a little before you go inside to clear your mind so you're focused only on what you want to focus on," Orpheus said, holding half of a blood bag for me to take. I emptied the contents into my eager mouth, letting the fragrant liquid run down my throat and satisfy the building hunger that never seemed to dissipate entirely.

Thanking him, I handed Orpheus the empty bag and pressed a gentle kiss against his lips. He groaned as the remnants of the blood on my lips graced his tongue, and he deepened the kiss. I barely gathered enough willpower to pull back from his embrace. I took a deep breath and gave Laz a slightly more reserved kiss before making my way up the driveway toward her door. My heart beat once, thumping foreignly against my chest in a way I hadn't felt since my transformation as I lifted my knuckles to tap on her door. It was nearly eleven at night, but I knew she would be up. She was a night owl at the best of times, but she became downright nocturnal when she was stressed. At least we had that in common now.

My knock echoed through her house, and my heightened hearing heard her moving around in her room, making her way toward the door. I glanced over my shoulder to where I had left my mates, but they were nowhere to be seen. I felt them close by, though, in the pulsing of our bond.

You've got this. We're here if you need us. Laz's voice echoed in my mind.

I still hadn't gotten used to that mental link I had created with my mates, but it quickly became my favorite part of this new existence. It eased a part of my anxiety and panic instantly. Something I had never quite had that kind of control over before. It felt empowering in a way I didn't realize I needed.

I love you. I whispered back through the channels of my mind and loved the answering warmth that flooded from Laz's mark on my skin. The phases of the moon just above my hip bone. Transformation. Change. Us.

The door opened, and I inhaled sharply, immediately worried my best friend would recognize that something about me had changed. She knew me better than I knew myself most times, and I wouldn't put it past her to see that I was hiding something the moment she laid eyes on me. There she was. Davia. Her blonde hair caught the light, her blue eyes wide with shock and relief. For a moment, time seemed to stand still. I had been so nervous for this reunion, terrified she would see through me, see the monster I had become. But as her eyes locked onto mine, all I saw was pure, unfiltered happiness.

"Athena!" she exclaimed, her voice a mixture of disbelief and joy. In an instant, she crossed the threshold and wrapped her arms around me, pulling me into a tight embrace. I hesitated, only slightly, as the scent of her blood invaded my senses. But her warmth and the familiarity of her scent, the real her, the one beyond the blood, overwhelmed me, and I allowed myself to melt into her hug.

"Oh my God, Athena, you're okay! I thought... I thought I'd lost you forever," she said, her voice cracking with emotion, a bizarre reaction for my normally stoic and hardheaded friend. She pulled back just enough to look at me, her hands gripping my shoulders. "Where have you been? What the fuck happened to you?"

I swallowed hard, forcing a smile. "It's a long story, Davia. But I'm here now. I'm okay."

She didn't seem to notice the subtle changes in me, the way my eyes no longer held the same warmth or how my skin was cooler to the touch. She was too relieved, too overjoyed to question anything. She only saw her friend back from whatever horrors she had concocted in her mind.

"I was so fucking worried," she continued, tears streaming down her cheeks. "Get in here," she said, ushering me into her living room. I smiled and followed behind her, thankful she invited me in without me needing to ask her to. Allowing relief that she was seemingly untouched by the Hunters to wash over me. That was yet another horrible possibility that I hadn't let myself think about, but now that she was here in front of me and safe, I let the fear I'd been harboring for my best friend drift away.

Davia led me to her couch, setting me down and plopping down right in front of me, her fingers intertwined with mine.

"Are you ok?" She asked, her eyes scanning my body for injuries. I prayed she didn't look too closely, or she'd see the raised white lines of my mate bonds, but I wasn't quite ready to explain that.

"I'm okay, I promise. I'm okay now."

She waited for me to continue, and here I was, finally arriving at the crossroads I knew was coming. I could tell her the story I told the police. All very rational, and honestly, knowing my history with abuse, she wouldn't question it for a moment. Or I could tell her the truth. The entire dark, dirty, scary, supernatural truth.

"Athena, what the hell happened?"

I met her eyes, full of worry and confusion. I needed to make a choice. Let her in on this secret and hope it doesn't paint a target on her back or keep this massive part of myself from her.

"I'm going to tell you something, and it's going to sound absolutely insane, and I need you to believe me anyway. Can you do that?" I asked, gripping her hands in mine. Her skin felt like a blazing inferno compared to mine.

"What are… I don't understand what's going on?" She shook her head.

"Can you promise me that you'll hear what I'm about to say with an open mind?" I slid forward on the couch until my knee brushed against hers.

"You're starting to scare me, Athena," she said, narrowing her eyes at me.

"I'm pulling the Vagina card," I blurted out, and her mouth dropped open as her eyes widened in shock. I met her gaze as the gravity of the weird girl-code contract was enacted. She nodded solemnly, seemingly accepting my terms.

"Okay," I started, leaning back and taking a long breath. This was going to be difficult. "I'll start at the beginning."

It came out as a torrent of emotional sobs, and I even started with the easy part. I told her the truth about what Louis tried that night at the bar, and I could barely see through my own tears enough to see her cheeks stained with moisture as well. Her hand clasped mine as she let me continue. I told her how my Wanderers saved me that night, how they got me home safe. I told her how Greg confronted me about the brick through the window and then the fight in the bookstore. I could feel her seething with fury about her old fling and what he was capable of.

Then, it was time for the hard part.

"This is where I need you to trust me," I prefaced, taking a long, steadying breath. "The reason I came to stay with you, the reason I needed some space from them was because…" I paused. "Fuck, this is going to sound crazy."

She leaned forward, bringing her forehead to mine. "I'm here, I'm listening, I hear you. Just tell me whatever it is. I already believe you."

I squeezed her hand and relished in the moment of intimacy shared with my best friend. I didn't realize how much I missed her when I was locked away until now. She meant so much to me, and I was so thankful I had her here in my arms now.

"I needed space from them because…because I found out they were vampires." The word slipped from my lips, and I loved how it felt on my tongue. It was a word that was just a fun thing I liked to read about and imagine at one point in my life, but now, it was everything to me. It was who I was.

I glanced up at Davia to gauge her reaction, but her face gave nothing away. I took that as an opportunity to continue. "They shifted in front of me and called me their mate. So I promptly freaked the fuck out and ran away." I giggled half-heartedly to lighten the mood. It didn't work. "I didn't want to believe it either, but it's true. They are vampires, and somehow, I am their mate. I belong to them, and they belong to me. We belong together." Whew, okay. I heard it. I was sounding like one of those wackos in the reality shows that people only ever really watched to see that they're relatively normal in comparison to the creeps on the screen.

"I don't understand," she said softly, which was a better reaction than expected.

"They've been on the run from vampire hunters for a while, and one of them actually found us…" this part was going to piss her off. Royally. I saw the way she looked him up and down, the glint in her eye that she only ever got when she liked what she saw. First Greg, then Archer. She was going to seriously freak out when she heard what he did.

"Archer was sent to kidnap them," I stated slowly. "So he did, and because he couldn't leave witnesses apparently, he took me too. That's where I've been for the last two weeks."

She blinked once. Twice.

"You were trapped in a vampire hunter's lair?" She repeated.

"Yes."

"After being kidnapped by a hunter?"

"Yes."

"Because the four people you're sleeping with are your fated vampire mates…"

"Yes."

She leaned back against the arm of the couch and exhaled deeply.

"Vagina card?" she clarified softly, an almost pleading look in her eyes. She wanted me to tell her this was all a joke. She wanted to laugh at my imagination, then kick my ass for scaring her. But I couldn't do that.

I nodded. "Vagina card."

"Well, shit," she whispered with a soft shake of her head. It sent golden tendrils of her hair spilling into her face. "You're kind of living my Twilight fan-fic dreams."

The laugh that bubbled out of my throat was two parts shock and one part utter relief. The pit in my stomach seemed to disappear, and I smiled gently at my best friend. I didn't realize how much tension I had been carrying in my body until the moment I could release it. As my muscles uncoiled and my shoulders relaxed, I felt refreshed. But then, the sickening thought occurred to me. She may have been willing to believe me, but would she accept me when she discovered that the monsters weren't just hypothetical anymore, but that I was one of them?

"There's more, isn't there?" She asked, recognizing the pained look on my face. I shrugged, exhaling quickly through my nose.

"You know how the only thing I've ever known about my father was his name?" I prompted, and she nodded. "He's one of the Hunters. He, um, he sent his son to capture us…" I waited for her to put the puzzle together quietly. It took a second. Her forehead creased as her brain sorted the new information into the appropriate categories.

"Holy shit," she said on a breathy exhale. "Archer is your brother?" I nodded. "And he kidnapped you because your father told him to?"

"Yeah."

"Talk about a fucked up family dynamic…" she said, shaking her head with a mixture of disbelief and shock.

"I know this is a lot - " I began.

"No, honey. My breakup last summer was 'a lot', but this is… god, this is on a completely different planet," she interjected.

"There's more." I chuckled darkly.

"Of course there is," she said, reaching forward to take my hand in hers again and squeeze it. "Go ahead, I'm here."

"When we escaped, my father sent Hunters to find us again. We fought, and they almost... They nearly killed.." I stopped, feeling the emotion bubble in my throat and the tears sting my eyes as I recalled the sickening panic that overtook me when I saw that they had Samara vulnerable. Davia's hand gripped mine tighter. "They almost killed Samara, and I couldn't just stand by and watch it. I had just found them, Davia. It sounds fast and unbelievable, but they are my family. They have a piece of my soul that I've been missing, and I couldn't lose that just when I found it. I didn't think about it. I just ran. If I could just get to her, I could do something. I could save her." Tears flowed down my cheeks. "I got to her, I threw myself in the way, and I was hurt."

I glanced up at Davia, trying to memorize the look on her face—concern, love, friendship. Just in case things shifted when she learned of my new development, I could remember this moment.

"I was going to die. Actually, I think I might have literally died there for a second."

Davia sniffled and used the back of her hand to wipe away the tears. "You're about to tell me that you're a vampire… aren't you?"

I scanned her features for any sign of fear or disgust, but all I saw reflected in her eyes was the same love and care with which I looked at her.

"Yeah," I whispered, letting my head fall forward so my eyes were locked on the couch. She touched my chin and raised my head to meet her gaze again.

"Athena Landry, I am your best friend. I noticed something was different with you the moment you walked in here." She held our joined hands up between us. "Your hands are like ice, your skin is annoyingly clear and perfect, and don't get me started on the tattoo-looking things all over you." She chuckled, and I followed suit.

"I may not…really understand what's going on here, and it's hard to believe for sure… but I'm here for you. I believe you, Athena. I love you. And nothing, supernatural or otherwise, could ever change the way I feel about you." Davia wrapped her arms around me and pulled me into a hug, and I melted into her embrace. My heart thumped loudly, bursting to life for a moment with the love I have for my best friend. When we pulled back from the hug, we met each other's eyes and then devolved into laughter.

"If you would have told little high school me about this, I'd probably have an even more dramatic and embarrassing vampire phase than I already did." She laughed, tucking a strand of hair behind her ear. "So, you like.. Drink blood now?"

I cringed. "Yeah, god, that's gross, isn't it?"

She shrugged. "How do I smell? Am I tempting?"

My shoulders shook with laughter. "Honestly, yes. But I just turned, so I think everyone is tempting right now."

"Can I see?" she asked timidly. I quickly bit my bottom lip to try and subdue the pointed fangs that desperately wanted to descend at the promise of blood.

"I'm not completely controlled yet," I replied, ashamed.

"I trust you," she said, offering me her wrist. My eyes were immediately drawn to the blood that ran through her veins like a moth to the flame.

"It's, um, sort of intimate," I challenged, trying my best to force the shift back. I didn't want to terrify her, or worse…kill her.

"Like a sex thing?" She asked, an eyebrow arched in amusement. I hid my head in my hands in embarrassment.

"Not always," I argued exasperatedly.

"Okay then, then take a little sip of La Rosé Davia." Davia took a deep breath and held her wrist to me again, her pulse visibly quickening under her skin. "Show me, please," she said softly, her voice steady despite the tremor I could sense beneath it. I hesitated, fear gnawing at me. What if I lost control? What if I hurt her?

"Are you sure?" I asked, my voice barely above a whisper.

She nodded, her eyes unwavering. "I trust you."

With a shaky breath, I let the shift, which was nearly at the surface, take over. My vision sharpened as my eyes turned red, my ears elongated to points, and my fangs bared themselves. I saw the flicker of surprise in Davia's eyes, but she remained calm outwardly. Her heartbeat, however, betrayed her nervousness, each thud sending a fresh wave of intoxicating scent through the air.

I gently took her wrist, feeling the warmth of her skin against my cool touch. The scent of her blood was overwhelming, far more potent than any of the blood from the bags that I had been surviving on since the transformation. I could feel my instincts clamoring for control, urging me to sink my fangs in deep and drink my fill. But I fought against that monstrous voice, reminding myself why I was doing this.

Slowly, I brought her wrist to my mouth and bit down gently, acutely aware of my new strength and trying not to cause her any harm. The instant her blood hit my tongue, I was flooded with warmth and life. It was unlike anything I had ever experienced. The blood from the bag had been a poor imitation—this was pure, rich, fragrant, and so *alive*. I had to force myself to take only a tiny sip, savoring the taste while battling the overwhelming desire to take more. My willpower was fighting for its life against the creature within me.

After what felt like both an eternity and a mere second, I pulled away, licking the minor puncture wounds on her wrist. To my relief, they closed almost immediately, leaving only a faint mark. I looked up at Davia, bracing myself for her reaction.

Her eyes were wide, filled with shock and incredulity. "I can't believe it," she whispered, her voice filled with awe. "That was incredible. And it didn't even hurt."

I let out a breath I hadn't realized I was holding, feeling a mixture of relief and exhilaration. "I'm glad you're okay," I said, my voice still shaky from the effort of restraint. "I was so scared I might hurt you."

Davia smiled, her eyes sparkling with a strange delight. "You didn't." She reached out, touching my face gently. "You're still you, Athena. Just a lot cooler now."

I laughed.

"Oh my god! We can go to goth night together!" Davia devolved into giddy planning mode, excitedly chatting about the different things we could do together now that I was 'less boring.' I sat back on my heels, listening to her, and felt a warmth spread through my chest.

My best friend believed me.

There was a time when she was one of the only ones who believed me when no one else would. I needed her support then, and I need it now.

I smiled as she droned on and on, and I knew I had made the right choice in divulging this secret to her. I'd let myself bathe in the warmth of this moment for as long as I could because soon, it would be time to speak to my grandmother.

And there'd be no giddy happiness in that discussion, so I'd soak it up now while I still could.

SILAS

TWO

"We're sunproofing, not preparing for an apocalypse," Samara said, slapping the sheets of wood out of my hands.

"Black-out curtains aren't gonna get the job done, or do you not remember the incident in Tuscon?" I challenged, and she shook her head.

"Of course, I remember Tuscon. My back was scarred for weeks."

I nodded, the memory of our early morning wake-up call the moment the sun rays spilled through the so-called 'black-out' curtains and burned into our skin.

"Then, this is what we need," I replied, reaching for the sheets of wood again.

"People are going to ask questions if Athena's house suddenly looks like she's prepping for a hurricane," Samara tossed back, pulling the sheets of wood from my grasp, putting them back on the rack, and pushing me out of the lumber aisle.

"Things have developed since the last time we had to sunproof a house," she argued while leading me to the window section of the store.

After an annoyingly extensive question-and-answer process with the employee, who was torn between wanting us to get the fuck out of his store because it was nearly eleven at night and wanting to make one hell of a commission on us, we had purchased three rolls of UV blocking window tint, and two sets of black-out curtains for each window.

After the walk, I stepped up to Athena's little cottage, and instantly, a thought occurred to me.

Hey, bookworm. You better invite me inside.

I felt her amusement through the bond.

Oh gosh, I don't know… I have a lot of valuable things inside…you know. She teased.

Don't make me punish you, baby girl. I taunted hungrily.

What if that's what I want? She answered, and I growled hungrily.

Let me in, baby girl, and I'll fuck you in your bookstore again. I promised. I planned on doing that again, no matter what, but it fits into our game so well.

Of course, you're welcome inside. Mi casa es su casa. Or whatever.

I chuckled, turning the handle and finding myself freely able to step over the threshold.

Do I get my reward soon, sir? She purred.

Fuck, yes. The minute we're alone, you're mine.

Good. She chuckled. *Hey, do I need to invite myself in when I get home?* She asked.

I have no idea. After I turned, I never went back to my old place. *I guess we'll find out soon.*

Stepping into Athena's little cottage was like coming home despite never even setting foot inside before. Archer was sitting awkwardly on the couch, not quite comfortable enough to get comfortable. I stood across the room, my gaze locking onto Archer's. There was a time when that look would have been filled with pure hatred. This was the man who had captured me, nearly destroyed everything I loved for fuck's sake. But now, things were different. Archer saved us and risked everything to do so, so my opinion of the little Hunter shifted.

I took a deep breath, feeling the familiar clench of my jaw before I forced myself to give Archer a slow, deliberate nod. It was a gesture that said everything

I wouldn't say aloud, a tentative acceptance of his place in Athena's - and, in turn, my - life.

Archer, standing from the couch, returned the nod with measured calmness. His expression was not smug or triumphant– just quiet understanding.

Samara, Archer, and I got to work quickly, quickly applying the window tint and replacing her cute, sage green curtains with dark, thicker curtains that would keep her alive and safe.

By the time we had finished, it was nearly one in the morning. Archer's mouth opened wide on a yawn, and I crossed the room to him.

"You should go get a room at the motel," I said.

"You kicking me out?" He teased on another yawn.

"Yeah."

His eyes widened in shock at my bluntness.

"Silas," Samara warned.

"Look, it's for your own good," I said, shrugging.

"My own good?" Archer confirmed.

"Yeah, look, this house isn't all that big, and I plan to make your sister scream my name as I pound my cock into her all night, so unless you wanna hear that, I suggest you go get a room," I responded flippantly.

Archer's face twisted in disgust, and he clamped his hands over his ears. "Oh Jesus, don't say shit like that to me." His body visibly shook as a chill ran through his body. Samara smirked and didn't scold me for my brash response. I knew she was just as desperate for our mate as I was. We hadn't spent a single moment alone together since we left the safe house. Not with her stupid brother tagging along the whole time.

"I'm just warning you," I answered. Archer nodded and headed toward the front door.

"I'll be back tomorrow afternoon. I'm going to try and get into contact with some of the Hunters that weren't complete asshats. I think they might listen if we tell them the truth. Tell Athena we can go talk to her grandma tomorrow night after sunset." He stepped across the threshold and disappeared into the darkness of night.

"You didn't have to be so blunt about it," Samara offered, settling onto the couch.

"Tell me you aren't glad he's gone," I challenged, raising a brow as I sunk into the armchair across from her. She shook her head and smiled softly.

"Of course I am. All I have been able to think about since she turned has been her sinking her fangs into my skin and finally marking me as hers."

I groaned, feeling my cock twitch to life at the thought.

Our mate bond is complete, but until she drank from us, we wouldn't bear the mark of her the way she carried ours. A desperate little thrill always filled me every time I saw my coiled serpents decorating her chest, and I couldn't wait to carry a piece of her with me. I needed her to mark me. I wanted her soul tattooed onto mine.

We finally had an eternity together. I wanted to make it count.

"So, you and Laz, huh?" she prompted softly, a little flustered. I met her eyes, searching for any signs of judgment or disgust.

"Only when Athena's involved," I responded, instantly feeling guilty. I wasn't ashamed about my attraction to Laz, and just because our connection was contingent on her involvement didn't make it any less important or intimate. "I mean... We're just, we're together when we are with her," I tried to explain, but I was doing a pretty shit job.

Samara leaned forward, a smile on her lips.

"About damn time."

Now, it was my turn to be flustered.

"What do you mean?" I asked.

"You two have had that intimacy building for as long as I've known you. I never thought it was sexual, just more connected than the rest of us, you know? You've always been the best to comfort each other. When you fight, it's passionate. When we lost Alora, they were the only one who could get through to you," Samara added quietly. I sighed. Every time her name was mentioned, my chest ached.

Losing Alora felt like a piece of my soul had been ripped away and shattered into a million pieces. She was my rock and confidant since childhood, the one person who always understood me, no matter what. We grew up together, facing the world side by side, and now she was gone. I felt lost and angry. So fucking angry. Nothing made sense without her. So I tried to find her in my vices. Danger, drink, drugs, draining… but she was gone.

Days turned into weeks into months, and the pain didn't lessen. It only grew, festering inside me like a fucking disease that was going to claim me. Samara, my partner in pain, seemed to begin to heal from the loss, but I couldn't. And I couldn't understand how she was suddenly okay after losing Alora. Did she even care to begin with? I pushed everyone away, retreating into myself, unable to face the world without Alora. Orpheus and Samara tried to talk to me, but their words felt hollow and meaningless.

Then there was Laz. They didn't try to offer empty platitudes or force me to talk about my feelings or my fucking grief. Instead, they simply sat with me, day after day, night after night, their presence a steady, calming force. At first, I didn't understand why it helped, but slowly, the weight of the loss and the pain began to feel more bearable when they were around.

Laz had a different kind of quiet strength about them, a way of making you feel seen and understood without saying a word. They would sit with me for hours, sometimes in silence, sometimes talking about nothing in particular. They gave me the space to mourn without judgment, and it was exactly what I needed.

One evening, as the sun dipped below the horizon, painting the sky in hues of orange and pink, Laz spoke softly. "Silas, it's okay to feel lost. But remember, you're not alone. We're all here for you whenever you're ready."

Their words broke through the fog of my grief, reaching a part of me I thought had been staked alongside Alora. I looked at Laz, really looked at them, and saw the sincerity in their eyes. They meant every word.

At that moment, something shifted inside me. The pain was still there, but it was no longer suffocating. Laz had given me a lifeline, a way to find my way back from the darkness. Slowly, I began to open up, to let them in. They didn't take Alora's place in my heart— no one ever could— but they carved out their own spot in my soul for themselves and helped me remember that life could go on and that I could find a new way to be okay.

"All I'm saying is that you two have a sort of understanding and love for each other that deserves to be explored. I'm happy for you," she finished, and I smiled at my friend.

"Thanks, Samara."

We sat in comfortable silence for a while, enjoying this brief moment of relative peace despite the cloud hanging over our heads, reminding us of the impending storm.

"The Hunters are going to be here any day now," I whispered the truth into the dark. I was so fucking sick and tired of those Hunters playing God. I couldn't wait to get my hands on this Dr. Kline asshole. I had spent a good portion of my time since learning his identity imagining all the ways I'd make him suffer for perpetuating the harm his great, great, great grand-whatever started when he created this fucking organization. I couldn't kill Jacob, as much as I wanted to, because vampire-hunting scum or not, he was Athena's father, and even though I knew she didn't hold any love for him, there's just something about family that changes things.

"I know," she replied.

"Do you think we have a chance?" I asked. She didn't answer right away. Instead, she placed her hand on her chest and smiled.

"With this bond?" She started. "I feel like anything is possible."

"I hope it is," I replied. I didn't want to admit it out loud, but I was terrified. Even more so than last time, Nameless had us in their clutches because this time, I had something even more important to me to lose. If I almost didn't survive losing Alora, I knew that losing Athena would mean the end of me.

No one ever truly wins a war, but I was determined to survive it with everyone I loved still with me.

My ears perked up at the sound of footsteps on the gravel driveway. Three sets. I stood up and waited for the rest of our coven to arrive. The door creaked open, and Athena poked her head in tentatively. Seeing her always seemed to take my breath away. I hoped I never got used to it.

Vampirism looked fucking good on Athena. She's still her. With wild red hair cascading like fire and eyes the same brilliant green that I'd been drawn to since I first saw her in that bar. But there's something different now, a quiet strength that came with her transformation, and it's nothing short of breathtaking.

I watched her from across the room as she entered her home, a new and changed person. I admired the way she carried herself despite the nerves.

I found myself captivated by her. She was beautiful before, a goddess with silky skin, but now she was stunning in a way that defied words. The transformation had brought out a new side of her, one that was both powerful and fucking intoxicating. Maybe it was that, or it also could be the fact that now I got to have her for eternity that made me feral for her.

Yet, beneath all that newness, she was still Athena. The same fire, the same fierce loyalty, the same heart. She glanced over at me as Orpheus and Laz followed behind her, catching my gaze, and smiled. That smile– it hadn't changed. It was the same one that had always made my heart race.

Athena walked over, and as she approached, I couldn't help but notice how the place in my chest where her bond sat burned brighter at her proximity. "What are you staring at?" she asked, a playful smirk on her lips.

"Just you," I replied honestly. "Vampirism looks good on you, bookworm. Really good."

She laughed softly, a sound that was music to my ears and made my cock twitch. "Thanks, Silas." She stood up on her tip toes to press a kiss on my cheek. I groaned at the touch. I was going to absolutely devourer this woman the moment I could. "I think I'm getting the hang of it."

"She drank from Davia and controlled herself beautifully," Laz interjected, pride lacing their tone.

"So you told her everything?" Samara asked.

Athena nodded.

"I had to. She's my best friend."

My heart ached slightly as Alora's face crossed my mind.

"You're stronger than ever, bookworm. And it's… fucking sexy," I teased, letting a hand drift down her waist to settle on her hips.

Her smile widened, and we just stood there for a moment, looking at each other. In her, I saw not just the vampire she had become but the incredible person she had always been.

I couldn't stand another moment of having her in my arms without tasting her lips, so I bent down to seal her mouth in a kiss. She made a short sound of shock but quickly sank into my kiss, and within a few seconds, our ravenous tongues were battling for dominance. Her hands gripped my hair and pulled, the force much greater than what she could have managed as a human, and it only made me harder for her.

"I need to fuck you," I whispered against her lips, and the moan she let out of downright sinful.

"Then do it already," she challenged, and without thinking, I tossed her over my shoulder and headed toward her bedroom. I glanced over my shoulder at the others.

"Are you coming or not?" I teased. I didn't care if Samara and Orpheus joined, I knew they preferred having Athena to themselves, but I needed Laz to come with me. I needed them to watch me make our girl scream, and I wanted to see them squirm as I told Athena how to please them.

I heard three sets of footsteps follow behind us as I stormed into her room and tossed my gorgeous mate down on her bedspread. Samara had the good sense to strip the bed and don fresh sheets while we waited and I was suddenly very thankful. I could not wait to defile them.

She gasped as her ass hit the bed, and I felt the bond in my chest tugging at her, desperate to be consummated by her fangs in my skin.

Soon. But not yet.

Orpheus settled on the chair in the corner of the room, legs spread wide as he sat like a watchful gargoyle. Stoic and rock hard. Samara leaned against the wall by the door with a lustful gaze. Laz, however, knew exactly what I needed from them. They came to a stop near the side of the bed, their hooded eyes bouncing between me and Athena.

"Laz, do you want to make our mate feel good?" I asked, my voice deep and husky.

"Yes, sir," they replied. Athena and I both released an almost feral moan as they submitted to me.

"Undress for us," I said. Us. Not her. This was just as much for me as it was for Athena, and I felt myself getting harder as Laz followed my command, slipping out of their pants and letting their shirt fall open and down their arms. Their cock jutted straight out, and I could see the glistening tip, wet with precum, and I had the surprising urge to dip down and taste it.

So I did.

Leaning over Athena, I brought my tongue to the tip of Laz's length and slowly trailed it along the slit. Laz threw their head back, and Athena whispered profanities as she watched me work. Laz's taste made me even more feral for the two of them than before. I slid their cock into my mouth and took it as far as I could, loving the way my mate beneath me pressed her thighs against my hips.

I pulled off of Laz with a wicked smile and stood up. Both of them were staring at me like I was the only thing in the world that mattered, like they would do anything for me. I wanted to test that.

"Baby girl, I need you to show me your perfect little pussy. Are you dripping for us?" She moved quickly, discarding her pants and underwear and leaving herself bare for me.

"Fuck," I exclaimed, unable to resist sliding my tongue through her perfect lips and drinking her arousal. She was soaking wet, and her hips bucked into my face as I tasted her.

"Laz, have a taste," I demanded, and Laz quickly slid to their knees at the foot of the bed. I stood behind them and watched as they devoured our mate's pussy. She thrashed wildly under their expert tongue, and I soaked up every second of the display as I quickly discarded my own clothes.

"Finger her ass Laz. We're going to take her together again, and I need her ready for me," I commanded, and Laz did as I asked, sliding a finger past the tight rim of muscles at her ass. She groaned their name, her hands tangling with the bedspread.

The sight was almost too sinful to see, and I was seconds away from spilling myself onto both of them. "Lay down on the bed, Laz." Athena whimpered when Laz withdrew their tongue and fingers, but he didn't dare complain.

Laz settled down beside her, their arms pressed against each other. They smiled sweetly at each other as they awaited my next instruction.

"Baby girl, I need you to ride them. Ride them until your cum is dripping down their cock."

Her eyes went wide, but she scrambled to obey. She went to straddle them, but I gripped her shoulders and directed her to face me.

"Eyes on me," I ordered. She nodded, settling in overtop of Laz. She looked back over her shoulder at them and smiled wickedly just before she sank down onto their cock. Watching the way their length stretched her pussy drew curses from the gallery of onlookers behind me. I knew that if I looked at Samara and Orpheus right now, I'd see lust and the darkest intentions painted on their faces, but I couldn't tear my eyes from the stunning creature in front of me.

Her mouth fell open with a gasp as she bounced up and down on Laz's dick. Laz held onto her hips and kept her pace steady and punishing. Just the way I knew she liked it. I leaned forward and took her clit into my mouth, and they both exhaled sharply with a moan as my tongue pleasured both her and them at the same time. It became a delicate dance. My tongue circled her clit, and dipped onto their cock, while Athena slammed her pussy down onto them. She cried out as an orgasm wracked through her body, sending shivers to every limb. I needed to be inside of my mate, and soon. I pulled her off of Laz and turned her so that her chest was pressed against theirs. I had the perfect angle to take Laz's cum soaked cock into my mouth, so I did. Savoring the way the two of them tasted together.

"Oh my god, Silas," Laz cried out.

Just then, I gripped Athena's hips and slid her down onto Laz's cock again. This time, as she rode them, I let my tongue soak the puckered hole that I was going to take to prepare her. When she was writhing in passion on Laz, I pressed the tip of my cock against her tight entrance and pushed my hips forward.

Otherworldly.

That's how it felt. Athena pressed back against me, taking me to the hilt like a fucking champ. Her muscles squeezed me like a vice, and I was seconds from coming and ending the whole thing. I reached around to grip her throat and pulled her up until her back was flush with my front. Laz and I continued to press into her from beneath as I whispered into her ear.

"Time to mark me, baby girl. Make me yours." With one hand holding her throat, I placed the other forearm in front of her mouth. Most of my arms were covered in ink, but there was a spot on my left forearm between two dark, inky patterns that had always been blank. I had always wanted to complete the sleeve, to find something that fit there, but nothing felt right. I should have known I was saving that spot for her. I pressed the patch of unblemished skin against her lips and groaned as her tongue darted out to taste it. Laz slowed their thrusts to allow us this moment, but the pressure of their length up against mine within our mate was deliciously torturous.

Athena's fangs descended and sank into my arm, and I threw my head back on a moan. Euphoria, unlike any I'd ever felt, flooded through my veins. She pulled mouthful after mouthful of my blood past her lips, and I squeezed harder with the hand around her throat. She gasped and pulled her fangs from my arm.

"Now kiss it all better," I demanded, my voice almost unrecognizable in the fog of lust. She stuck her tongue out and waited for me to press my arm against it again. She lapped up the remaining blood and sealed the wound with a little extra sensual flair. When I dropped both hands to her hips, she fell forward onto Laz, gasping for air.

"I think it's time to claim your next mate, baby girl. Claim them while I fuck your ass."

I pounded into her for a few moments, in tandem with Laz's thrust into her pussy. She cried out before pressing a kiss against Laz's throat. I slowed my thrusts, content to simply watch as two people I loved shared their love for one another.

Athena bit down onto Laz's throat, just above the shoulder, and the way she clenched around me should have been illegal. Laz's hands tangled in her hair, and I watched as she made her claim official. Sitting back, she licked the wound closed.

"Baby girl, you deserve a reward for that. Don't you think?" I teased.

She glanced at me over her shoulder, her green eyes shining wickedly. "Yes, sir. I do."

I made eye contact with Laz, a silent exchange, and then we unleashed. Our thrusts into her body were rough and punishing, and she took each slam of our cocks into her like she was made for it. I was so close, and my fingers dug into her hips as she rode us with reckless abandon. She reached her climax first, which only sent me spiraling after her. I came with her name on my lips, and I could feel Laz's thick cock pulse as they spilled into her as well.

I pulled out first, followed by Laz. I helped lay Athena down on the bedspread, and she sprawled out, sated and exhausted. Her perfect body was on display for us. I could see the evidence of our domination spilling from her perfect pussy.

I wanted more. Honestly, I never wanted to stop. But I knew that there were more mates that she needed to claim. I leaned over her and stole a kiss. She melted into it, clearly still riding high from her orgasm.

"It's their turn now, baby girl," I said, tilting my head toward the door and the chair in the corner where her other mates had been watching from. "Put on a good show for me," I demanded with another kiss before sliding off the bed and moving to the wall. Laz joined me, leaning just a few feet from me.

Samara's eyes scanned Athena's naked form, and she exchanged the briefest silent exchange with Orpheus before she rushed forward to join her mate on the bed. I thought I would hate to see the day Samara moved on with someone else. I thought it would hurt to see her happy with someone else. But this was *right*. This was what Alora would have wanted for us. My dead heart felt alive as I watched my friend and my mate fall in love.

Samara wasted no time stripping off her dress and straddling Athena, pressing her dripping core against Athena's. The two of them made positively nasty sounds as they ground their cores against each other. I was so focused on watching the pleasure on my mate's face that I didn't even notice that Laz had slipped a hand around my waist and was leaning their body weight into mine. It felt nice. I held them close and watched Samara bring our mate to another screaming orgasm, and it felt almost… perfect.

I'd do anything to keep this family safe. Anything.

ORPHEUS

THREE

Athena's fangs sunk into Samara's chest, just above her breast, and I watched with rapt attention as they both came from the sensation. Watching Athena come undone repeatedly proved to be the most challenging test of my willpower, but if I waited, it meant I got her all to myself. As Samara and Athena exchanged whispered admissions of love, I slid my pants off and let them pool on the floor by my feet and let my button-down fall from my form and bunch at my waist. My cock was so hard I was afraid that even the slightest touch would have me erupting.

Samara slid off the bed and smiled at me as she slid her dress back over her head. Athena watched her, thoroughly enjoying the view. "Are you ready for me, little nymph?" I asked, drawing her attention to me.

Her lips were tainted red from the blood she had consumed, and they looked delicious as she drew her bottom lip between her teeth and nodded coyly.

"Come to me," I whispered. My eyes remained glued to her as she slid from the bed and approached me. Her lips were plump, and her hair was wild. She looked freshly fucked, and god, that thought turned me on even more. I never thought I'd share a woman with my coven, but this woman deserves every ounce of pleasure my coven can give her and then some. I couldn't wait to give her all of me.

"Climb up here and sit on my face," I ordered her, leaning my head back on the back of the armchair. She didn't hesitate and climbed up my body to rest her core above my willing mouth. "Sit. Down." I demanded. She pressed her core down against my face, and my tongue dove into her folds, lapping up the collective taste of my coven's arousal. She rocked wildly against my face, and I growled, using my hands to encourage her as she aggressively sought out her orgasm against my tongue. Her hands tangled in my hair as I sucked her clit into my mouth.

"Orpheus!" She cried out, her body tensing as another climax claimed her. I let her ride out the orgasm on my mouth, then helped her slide down my form until she straddled me on the chair. A leg on either side, my erect cock pinned between our bodies.

"I need you to mark me, Athena. I need to wear your imprint on my body."

Her green eyes met mine in a silent exchange, then she nodded, lifting her core until she could sink onto my cock. I groaned as she stretched around me. Her body was perfectly crafted to fit mine, and the moment she sank her teeth into my throat, time seemed to slow to a crawl. Every sensation was heightened, every nerve ending alive with electric energy. Her lips were soft against my skin, her breath warm and teasing before her fangs broke through. The pain was sharp, but it quickly dissolved into something more profound and deeply intimate.

I felt a rush of overwhelming exhilaration as she began to drink. Our connection deepened with each pulse of my blood into her mouth, strengthing the bond that already sat steadfast in my chest. The world around us faded, leaving only the two of us entwined in this intimate and perfect moment.

Her hands gripped my shoulders, grounding me as the euphoria intensified. It was sinfully sensual, the way she moved against me, the way her touch sent shivers down my spine. I could feel her single heartbeat align with mine, our breaths synchronizing as if we were becoming one.

I closed my eyes, surrendering entirely to the sensation of her. The mark she was leaving on me, her mate mark, was more than just a physical imprint– it was a declaration, a promise of forever– an eternity.

As she pulled back, her tongue traced the wound, sealing it with a gentle, almost loving caress. I opened my eyes to find her staring at me, the green orbs glowing with a mix of satisfaction and something deeper, something that mirrored my own devotion.

"You're mine now," she whispered, her voice a soft, intimate murmur that sent a new wave of warmth through me.

"I already was," I whispered back before bucking my hips up into her and bringing both of us back to the edge of a climax. I circled her clit with my finger, and within a few more thrusts, we were falling apart together. A mess of love, limbs, and lust.

As our breathing returned to normal, she chuckled. Sitting there, still wrapped in each other's embrace, I felt a profound sense of belonging. I was marked, I was hers, and nothing had ever felt so right.

Her eyes drifted closed, so I helped her up, and the four of us quickly got her cleaned up and ready for bed. The night of our last mate bond joining had been unfairly cut short, but this time, we would savor this night with her. Each of us now had a brand new mark. Thin raised white lines that decorated our skin, shaped like something so perfectly Athena it could have been nothing else.

A rose.

I smiled at the tiny mark that now permanently decorated my skin and the skin of my coven and recalled how Silas had demanded to get a bouquet for her before the tour that changed everything. She's always been our perfect rose. And now we had the mark to prove it.

The five of us carefully and uncomfortably slid between her bed sheets.

I made a mental note to get us a larger bed if this was going to be the norm. There, holding Athena against my body while her other mates pressed in as well, all of us, healthy, safe, sated… I sincerely hoped it would be.

ATHENA

FOUR

I was curled up on the couch, staring at the covered window. It was midday, but you wouldn't know it from inside here. The sun was a distant memory, and the darkness felt all-consuming, even though it was supposed to be a protective cocoon. I missed the sun's warmth on my skin, the way it used to fill me with energy and light. I missed my bike rides in the wee hours of the morning just as the sun's rays started to peek out over the horizon. Now, I was just grumpy and tired of being confined to the night.

"This sucks," I muttered to myself, drawing my knees up to my chest.

The others thought my grumpiness was cute, but it didn't change the fact that I was miserable. I wanted to go to New Orleans to find the vampire who could give me resistance to the sun. I needed it, and I needed it soon. The thought of spending another day like this, shrouded in darkness, made my sun-sensitive skin crawl.

Laz wandered into the room, their eyes twinkling with amusement as they took in my curled-up form. "You look like a disgruntled kitten," they said, plopping beside me and ruffling my hair.

I huffed, swatting their hand away. "I feel like one, too. I'm tired of being nocturnal. I want to feel the sun again."

Samara joined us, her laughter soft as she settled on my other side. "Patience, love."

"You're so cute when you're grumpy," Silas teased, sliding his hand along my cheek. I pulled my head back and crossed my arms over my chest in a huff, which only drew more laughter from my amused mates.

Orpheus leaned against the doorway, his gaze warm and understanding. "We'll go to New Orleans as soon as we can. Don't let the other's tease you. They were chomping at the bit to feel the sun again, too." He smiled at me, then sighed. "We will prioritize it the moment we are all safe. I understand the loneliness of the dark."

I sighed, the frustration still bubbling under the surface but soothed slightly by their presence and the guilt that I'd only been nocturnal for a few days while Orpheus had spent a century confined to the darkness. "I'm sorry. I know I'm whining, and you all had to do it for much longer than I have. I shouldn't complain."

Silas turned to me, his eyes full of sympathy. "You're still allowed to be upset, bookworm. In the meantime, maybe we can find something to distract you from your grumpiness."

I rolled my eyes, but a small smile tugged at my lips. "Fine, but nothing dirty, ok? My body needs three to five business days to recover from what you all did to me last night."

They all laughed, the sound filling the room with warmth I couldn't get from the sun. For now, that would be enough.

"You know, I wouldn't be surprised if your vampire gifts get an upgrade as well after you marked us," Laz said, smiling.

"Really?" I replied, shocked. My gift was already so powerful I didn't know how it could get any better.

"They're right," Orpheus chimed in. "We each had our latent gifts upgraded, so it would be logical to assume yours would, too."

"What do you think it'll be?" I asked the room.

"Have you felt anything change with your gift today?" Silas urged.

No, it feels the same. I replied via the channels of my mind.

Silas nodded.

"Well, give it time. Mine didn't manifest until I needed it," Laz promised. I nodded quietly, my eyes closed, taking a moment to analyze the strange gift that had settled into my mind since my transformation. It felt like a physical presence, something tangible nestled deep within my consciousness. It wasn't just the mate bond that connected me to Laz, Samara, Orpheus, and Silas– it was something more unique.

This ability to communicate with them wasn't like the telepathic links I'd read about in books or seen in movies. It was different, more intimate. It worked in tandem with the mate bond, wrapping around it like ivy climbing up a tree, using it as a vessel for our thoughts and emotions.

I focused on the sensation, feeling the connecting threads to each of them. The bond with Silas was vibrant and playful, tinged with his unique spark of energy. Samara's bond was deep and soothing, a well of calm and wisdom. Orpheus's connection was passionate and intense, like an eternally simmering fire. And Laz's bond was strong and steadfast, grounding me with their unwavering presence.

I tried to experiment with the gift and sense any additional factions or unique changes. But it all felt the same. Frustrated, I sent out a tentative thought, trying to pull on all four bonds simultaneously.

Can you hear me?

Almost immediately, I felt the responses. Laz's laughter echoed in my mind, followed by a playful, *Loud, and clear darlin'.*

Samara's voice was a gentle caress. *Yes, we're here.*

Orpheus's reply was a warm surge of affection. *Always.*

Silas's presence wrapped around me like a comforting embrace. *We're all with you.*

I took a deep breath, marveling at my mind's intricate web of connections. This ability was a part of me now, an extension of the bonds I shared with my mates. And maybe soon, it might be something more– something that could help us defeat Nameless and begin our lives without fear.

Opening my eyes, I looked around at my mates, scattered throughout the room but connected to me in a way that defied physical distance. I sent out another thought, this one filled with gratitude and love. *Thank you for being here with me and for being a part of me.*

Their responses came in the form of soft smiles.

"I can talk to all four of you at the same time. Maybe that's the upgrade?" I mused out loud.

"Did you try to do that before?" Orpheus inquired.

I thought about it. In the few days since the transformation, I had only ever really tried to speak to one of them at a time. So, I could have done that already, but I just didn't realize it.

"No," I huffed. Laz smiled, patting my head like the disgruntled kitten they assumed me to be.

"Don't worry. If you're going to get something additional, it'll come when you need it most," Orpheus promised.

A knock on the door made us jump to our feet in fear. I hadn't heard any footsteps leading up the driveway, and according to their reaction, my mates hadn't either. I quickly realized in this new life that not many people have the skills to sneak up on a vampire. Unless, of course, they're trained for it.

"Get in the other room, Athena," Silas ordered in a rushed whisper, standing up to face the door, his back tense and rigid.

"I can help!" I whispered. "I'm stronger now."

"Not when the door is open and the sun floods in," Samara reminded me, and I groaned internally before retreating around the corner. My mates prepared themselves and headed toward the door. My heart felt like it wanted to race if it could. Orpheus shifted, letting his vampiric form overtake his human features. His eyes darkened, his ears tapered off to a point, his nails elongated, and his posture became more rigid as his body transformed. I wondered briefly how I looked fully shifted. I was so afraid the first time I saw them like this. So scared of the "monsters" in my bookstore. But now, I didn't see a monster. I saw my protectors and my mates in all their supernatural glory.

Orpheus opened the door, and I slid behind the corner of the wall, instantly feeling a burning warmth from the sun that peaked through the doorway. I tensed, feeling my fingernails dig into the wood on the archway where I was hiding.

"Holy shit!" Archer's surprised voice echoed through my little cottage, and I heard my mates visibly relax. A few moments later, Archer entered, albeit timidly, and the door was shut behind him.

I stepped out from my hiding space and met eyes with my terrified brother.

"You scared the shit out of me," Archer explained, panting and placing a hand on his heart. The elevated heart rate pounded across the room, beckoning me to the running blood within his veins, but I shook my head and forced the impulse away.

"How the hell did you get up to the house so quietly?" Silas sneered, running a hand through his hair.

"I'm used to approaching places silently. Occupational hazard, sorry," he said, holding his hands up.

The five of us took seats in the living room, the tension slipping away but not entirely disappearing. We'd never fully relax until the threat was gone.

"I have some updates," Archer started. I leaned forward, resting my elbows on my knees. "I reached out to a few of the Hunters from my class that I remember, a few that were less... eager to, you know, murder vampires." He winced, and my mates followed suit.

"On a secure line, I'm sure," Orpheus prompted.

Archer rolled his eyes. "Yes, I'm not an amateur."

"So, what did they say?" Silas interjected.

"Kinda ran the gamut, honestly." He shrugged. "A few of them laughed in my face. One person told me that I deserved to be 'staked like those blood-sucking leeches for turning coat.'" He said it so flippantly, but I could see how the words affected him. I reached across the way to place a hand on his. He smiled softly at me.

"Sounds like you made great progress," Silas teased. Samara elbowed him in the ribs, and he grunted.

"Did anyone hear you out?" Samara asked, hopeful.

"Yeah, actually." He nodded.

"How many?" Orpheus urged.

Archer looked down at his hands and played with his fingers idly. "One."

Silas groaned and leaned back, and I felt myself lose any ounce of hope I had allowed myself to feel.

"She won't be able to convince anyone else, but she said she'd feed me intel when she could," Archer announced eagerly.

"That's useful, thank you, Archer," Orpheus asserted.

"She told me that my father hasn't been seen at HQ since yesterday morning," Archer confessed in a whisper. We all knew what that meant. He was on his way, and he'd be here soon.

"Ok, we already knew they'd be on their way. We were ready for that kind of news." Samara tried to sound optimistic, but it fell a little flat.

"She also said that Dr. Galvin was rumored to be coming out of hiding to join him on this hunt." That had all of us holding our breath.

On the journey back to Shockgrove, my mates and brother had let me in on all they had been able to gather about him, which, frustratingly, wasn't much. Galvin was never seen without a mask, a Nameless Hunter staple, but even at Nameless functions, he remained elusive, like a shadow in the night. There was no history about him on the internet past fifteen years ago.

Archer told me everything he knew about him from his time there. Apparently, a member of the Galvin family had been at the head of Nameless since its inception, passed down like some twisted family heirloom. Instead of a watch or a quilt or something, it was a vampire-hunting organization—a legacy of blood and death.

Laz had dug deep on the internet, using every resource, but Dr. Kline Galvin was a ghost. There were whispers and rumors, but nothing concrete. No one knew what he looked like under that mask, and it seemed like he preferred it that way. His true identity was a closely guarded secret even within the Nameless Hunters.

After a mission went south, he had been in hiding for a while. Archer didn't know how long precisely. He hadn't seen him since his graduation day. The day they branded him. I had felt sick to my stomach when he told me about that– marked by the twisted, burning metal and claimed as an agent of death and persecution. I offered to buy him a tattoo to cover it. He seemed interested in that idea.

This mysterious fog surrounding him was infuriating. How could someone so integral to the Nameless Hunters' operations be such an enigma? Knowing that we were up against someone who had managed to remain hidden for so long, someone who operated in the shadows and pulled the strings from behind the scenes, made me uneasy. Information is power, and we had none.

I glanced at my mates, each absorbed in their thoughts. They were just as frustrated as I was. Dr. Kline Galvin may have been a ghost, but he was on his way to haunt us, and we needed to be prepared for anything.

"We will be ready for them," Orpheus assured.

"How can you be so sure?" I stuttered.

Orpheus met my eyes and moved to kneel before me. His fingers caught my chin and tilted my head to kiss my lips. "Because have you ever known me not to have contingency plans?"

I smiled. "I haven't known you that long, actually," I teased.

"Really? See, I think I've known you for my entire life," he whispered softly, letting his lips dust against mine for another gentle kiss.

"I love you," I confided in a breathy moan against his lips.

"Love is only part of what I feel for you," he proclaimed softly before sitting back and addressing the group. "I have a plan to help us should we need it. It's a long shot, but I figured if there were ever a time to take a risky shot, it would be now."

"What did you do?" Silas asked.

"I called for backup," he declared.

I stared at Orpheus, my mind reeling from his words. "You called for backup?" I asked, trying to wrap my head around it.

He nodded, his expression calm. "Yes, we may need reinforcements."

"More vampires?" I probed, my voice barely above a whisper.

"Among others," he replied casually as if it were the most natural thing in the world.

"No," Silas growled.

"Yes," Orpheus replied.

"What's going on?" I asked, looking between the two of them.

"You called Elias?" Silas asked, utter disbelief coloring his tone. I glanced at my mates, who were wearing equally shocked looks.

"He owes us." Orpheus shrugged.

"But then we'll owe him, and do you really want to make that asshole another promise?" Silas bellowed. "I just barely survived the last one!"

"That was entirely different. If my coven is alive and safe, I'll make him any promise he wants."

His words sounded almost muddled as my brain swam with the introduction of this new knowledge. I knew logically there had to be other vampires out there– our kind couldn't be limited to just us– but we had never talked about it. The world of the supernatural had always seemed like a small, contained bubble around my mates and me. Now, with Orpheus' simple statement, that bubble had burst, revealing a vast, intricate web of beings I hadn't even begun to comprehend.

My mind raced. What did he mean by 'among others'? Were there other supernatural creatures out there? Werewolves? Witches? Things I hadn't even imagined? The possibilities seemed endless and overwhelming.

I looked at Orpheus, searching his eyes for answers. "What do you mean, 'others'?" I asked, my voice tinged with curiosity and apprehension.

He gave me a reassuring smile. "Well, if they come, like I hope they will, you'll see soon enough. The supernatural world is much bigger than you think, Athena. Nameless may have dwindled our numbers, but we may not have to be alone in this fight."

I nodded slowly, trying to process this new reality. The shock was starting to give way to a strange sense of anticipation. There was so much more to learn and to understand about this hidden world I was now a part of.

The realization was both daunting and exciting. My life had already changed so dramatically since becoming a vampire, and now it seemed there were even more changes on the horizon. I took a deep breath, steeling myself.

"We need to talk to your grandma to figure out what she knows," Archer insisted, and I felt my stomach twist with pain.

"I'm scared," I confessed.

Samara placed her hand on my back and ran a comforting hand along my spine. My back relaxed slightly under her touch.

"We'll be there to protect you," Laz promised.

"She's at your shop. I walked past earlier today just to check it all out. The sign said she'd be there until close. So, we can probably catch her if we head out as soon as the sun sets," Archer suggested, and my mates all nodded their heads.

The sun would set in a few hours, and I would finally have to face the truth. I hoped I could hold it together.

*

After the sun finally set, casting long shadows across the ground, we made our way to the pier. I stood at the spot where everything had changed. It was here that I had struggled against Greg, where he had placed his vicious hands on my body and tried to make me submit. It was here where I fought back, and he slipped away into the churning waves below. The memory of that, the fear and desperation, still lingered, but tonight, something else was gnawing at me– was he still out there? I turned away from the railing where Greg was last seen and headed down the quiet pier toward The Maine Plotline. It had been more than two weeks since I had seen it, since that day when Greg had found me there, and everything had spiraled out of control.

The window was fixed now. It felt strange to see the updated visage of the store, so new and pristine when the scars of that night remained etched onto my soul and probably always would. As I approached, I saw Grandma inside, her silhouette moving between the bookshelves. She had been keeping secrets from me, and now, more than ever, I felt the weight of those hidden truths.

The quaint bookstore, once my home away from home, now felt tainted with memories of violence and betrayal. It used to be my refuge, a place where I had found solace among the pages of countless stories. But now, standing outside, for the first time, I didn't want to go inside.

You've got this. Laz promised in my mind.

Taking a deep breath, I pushed open the door and stepped into the suddenly unfamiliar warmth of The Maine Plotline. The scent of books and old wood enveloped me, soothing yet tinged with unease. Grandma looked up from behind the counter, her expression a mix of relief and concern as she saw me. Her eyes flicked to my mates who stood behind me, but she didn't seem afraid or concerned.

"Athena," she said softly, setting aside the book she had been holding. "You're back. You're okay."

I nodded, trying to muster a smile. "Yeah, I'm back." But I certainly wasn't okay.

Her eyes scanned the people at my back. Did she know everything? Did she know who they were? What they were? How much of my connection was shared with her by my father?

Silence hung heavy between us, filled with unspoken words and unanswered questions. I didn't know where to start. My eyes drifted over to the counter. A vase filled with pink roses looked back at me. I felt warmth in my bonds as I saw them.

"I kept them alive for you," she whispered. I took this moment to really study her. The last few weeks had done little to help her health. In fact, she looked worn and tired. Guilt gripped my heart. I hated that I had worried her, that I had forced her to deal with all of this alone, without even knowing if I was alive. Her soft grey hair was pulled back into a braid that traveled down her back. Her floral patterned dress flared out at her feet, and she wore a shawl that gave her an almost Stevie Nicks look. But despite the colorful appearance, her eyes were dull and hollow. Clearly, worry had gotten the best of her.

She came around the counter, her steps hesitant as she approached me. "I'm so sorry, Athena," she said, her voice thick with emotion.

I swallowed hard, the lump in my throat threatening to choke me, before throwing my arms around her neck and pulling her into an embrace. She gasped as she met my icy frame but sunk into the hold. "I know," I whispered. "But now... now I need to know everything."

She nodded, pulling back. Her eyes were filled with a mixture of guilt and determination. "Come," she said, gesturing towards the back of the store where we could talk in private. "Archer, close up the front, will you?" She tossed toward my brother. Did she know who he was to me? Or did she still consider him the friendly stranger I made friends with? "Let's sit down. There's much we need to discuss."

We moved towards the back of The Maine Plotline, my mates following behind, toward where the cozy reading nook I'd spent that evening with Silas awaited us. Soft string lights hung delicately above, casting a warm, amber glow that bathed the area in a comforting light. Ivy vines crawled along the ceiling and draped over the shelves, adding a touch of natural beauty to the cozy space. The plush green velvet couch beckoned invitingly in the corner of the nook, and flashes of all the ways Silas claimed me returned to my mind.

Reminiscing, baby girl? Silas purred into my mind, and I fought off the blush.

Behave. I warned and earned an outward chuckle from him. My other mates glanced his way, but he just shrugged and smiled at me.

Grandma led me to one of the armchairs, its velvet cushions sinking slightly under my weight as I settled in. She sat opposite me on the couch, her expression serious yet tinged with a hint of warmth. Laz and Samara took seats on the open furniture while Silas and Orpheus stood to the side. Archer followed after locking the front door and claimed a seat on the hardwood floor.

As we sat there, the faint scent of old paper and coffee lingered in the air, mingling with the quiet rustle of pages as Grandma reached for my hand. Her touch was reassuring, grounding me in the present moment as she prepared to reveal the truths that had been hidden from me.

She searched my eyes for confirmation that I was prepared for what she was about to divulge. I nodded, my throat tight with emotion. "I'm ready," I replied, my voice steady despite the uncertainty that lay ahead.

"Okay," she began. "I think it's important to start at the beginning and let you know that your father and mother honestly loved each other very much while they were together." My shock must have shown on my face because she quickly added, "I know that's hard to believe considering how little she discussed him, but her opinion of him was colored by how he left, not the love they shared while he was here."

Her eyes filled with a sadness that I only ever saw when she was discussing Mom.

"Jacob Bennett was a good man when I knew him, but he had… unique opinions about the world. Franny tried to see past it," she uttered.

"What kind of opinions," I prompted.

She steadied her breathing. "He believed in the supernatural and in a much more serious capacity than me, believing I can feel your grandfather's spirit sometimes."

I watched her to gauge her reaction. Did she know just how accurate he had been?

"Okay," I said quietly.

"At first, your mother thought it was just a hobby, but it turns out he was part of some organization that was really immersed in that sort of world."

Archer shifted uncomfortably on the floor.

"So, she didn't believe him and kicked him out?" I asked. I needed to know how much she knew.

"No, no. It's a little more complicated than that. He showed her the truth, convinced us that creatures of the night did exist, and they were dangerous."

My mates bristled. I felt the bond in my chest tug as they pulled on it for strength.

"So, you believed in what he was saying?" I asked.

She nodded. "If you'd seen what I had, you would too." I thought back to the office where I was held and the photos Archer had shown me. I wondered if she had seen any of those. Had they been enough to convince her? They might have worked on me had I not already known who my Wanderers were.

"Your father was trying to eradicate the monsters and keep us all safe," she said, and I felt my mates tense at the term. "Franny didn't see it that way."

"What do you mean?"

"You know your mother, she was always a bleeding heart. There wasn't a creature alive she didn't empathize with." She smiled softly as she spoke of her. "She thought your father was just as bad as the creatures he hunted. He thought she was crazy. They fought. When she found out she was pregnant, she gave him an ultimatum. He could renounce his obsession with killing monsters or leave the two of you and never come back."

I felt the hollow pain in my chest intensify. He had chosen his anger and his obsession over being my father. It stung more than I cared to admit. Tears began to pool in my eyes.

"She was broken when he left. I mean, I've never seen her in so much pain. She was pregnant and just had her heart shattered," her voice caught in her throat. I hated the thought of my mother feeling like that. "When you came along, you put the pieces back together."

I felt my mates caressing my bond, comforting me as the new information came in.

"She wanted nothing to do with him. She never wanted you to know him. So, when he wouldn't stop calling to hear about how you were, I saw how it broke her. Each time the phone rang, her smile would drop, and she would retreat into her shell. Eventually, I couldn't take it anymore, so I answered the phone. She didn't know, of course. I was going to tell him off, tell him to leave us alone if he knew what was good for him. But he asked about you, and I could hear it in his voice." She paused, taking a breath. "He was misguided, a downright fool, but he cared about you. I told him you were okay just to get him to stop calling." A mixture of complicated feelings swirled in my stomach at that thought. He cared enough to see how I was, but not to stay? "But then he kept calling me, kept asking about you, and damnit, I couldn't cut him off from you."

We were both crying.

"Now, I think it's your turn to tell me what the hell you meant when you said he had you kidnapped. Because the Jacob Bennett I knew would never do such a thing to his daughter."

I took a deep breath, looking over at Archer, who offered me a soft nod.

"You know the monsters that he hunts?"

Her eyes narrowed in suspicion, but she nodded.

"Well, I am one of those creatures," I admitted into the darkness.

"What?" She stuttered, leaning away from me.

"I am a vampire, Grandma," I declared. She shook her head, studying me as if she was trying to note the differences.

"No, that's not…" her eyes drifted over to Orpheus, then Silas, Samara, and Laz, finally landing on Archer.

"Is this them? The Wanderers?" She asked softly, and I held my gasp in just barely. I felt Orpheus tense, and Silas' knuckles were white from just how tightly he clenched his fists.

"*We* are The Wanderers," I admitted for the first time out loud, although it had been the truth long before the transformation ever occurred.

She sighed, placing her head in her hands.

"Your father told me about them. He told me what to look for and the warning signs that a vampire might be nearby. After that boy from the Craving Crab went missing, I told him I thought they might have been here in Shockgrove…I didn't know…"

"You didn't know that he would kidnap us and try and kill us?" I finished.

She inhaled sharply, her response getting stuck in her throat, but ultimately nodded her agreement.

"Well, he did." I wasn't angry with her. She was operating under the only side of truth she was given, it wasn't her fault, but I couldn't help but feel betrayal seep into my bones.

"Athena," she started. "I'm so sorry. I was just trying to keep you safe."

I knew that. I did. And one day, I'd forgive all of this. I was sure of it. But the sting was so fresh that I couldn't shake it yet.

"Will you introduce me to your friends?" She asked timidly, and my eyes shot up to stare at her.

"You mean it?"

"If they're important to you, they're important to me, too."

"I don't know," I began timidly. "Their stories are theirs to tell." Laz noticed my hesitation and stepped in.

"My name is Laz, ma'am. It's a pleasure to meet you." They really laid on the charm as they tipped their head to my grandma. "I was turned into a vampire after a bunch of bigots in my town decided they'd rather I be dead than queer. Samara saved my life by turning me. Gave me a chance to live long enough to become who I truly was." My grandma listened intently to their words. Tears still flowed from her eyes.

"I was a victim of the LA Times bombing," Silas added. "If Orpheus didn't turn me, I wouldn't have made it."

"My parents used to sell my body to the highest bidder," Samara revealed. My breath caught in my throat. I knew her story wasn't a happy one, but hearing it in such plain terms felt sickening. My grandma felt the same.

"Oh honey…" grandma whispered.

"Orpheus found me one night, and he paid my fee but asked for nothing in return." She smiled over at Orpheus, who looked at her with such love and care that my dead heart nearly burst. "He paid my fee every night for a month. Giving me what I needed to satisfy my parents without forcing me to give away any more pieces of myself."

My grandma placed a hand on her heart as she listened.

"He offered me a way out of that. He gave me my life back."

I love you. I whispered to her via our mental link and felt her tug on the bond in response. Warmth spread through my veins.

"I don't know who turned me," Orpheus interjected. He remained stoic, standing gently against the bookshelf. "I woke up in this new existence completely alone. I struggled, trying to control my thirst and find my place in this world. I was on my own for… a really long time." I heard a slight crack in his voice, which made my heart ache. "Then I found Samara, and then Laz and Silas… and suddenly I had a family again."

He turned his eyes to me.

"And when we found Athena, our whole lives, every ounce of pain, every threat we faced, all the persecution…it was all worth it because finally we had the one thing we had been missing."

"We love your granddaughter, Miss Landry," Laz added.

"We would do anything to protect her, keep her safe, and make her happy," Samara said, smiling warmly at me.

"She's everything to us," Silas pledged like a vow.

My grandma's eyes were full of emotion as she looked around the room at my mates. They landed on Archer. "And you? Are you one of her… partners, too?"

"No!" Both Archer and I shouted simultaneously. Grandma jumped slightly, startled by our adamant denial.

"No, we're not together," I insisted, struggling to keep the disgusting mental image away. "He's Jacob's son."

She gasped, pressing her hand to her mouth. "Oh my word," she started. "You're.."

"Athena's brother," Archer finished.

"You look just alike…I should have seen it," she mused breathily, looking between us. "Are you also a…"

"No, ma'am. I worked with my father until recently. I realized I couldn't stay there when they showed me the truth." He indicated to my mates.

"He helped us escape," I added. She didn't need to know he kidnapped us, to begin with. He felt guilty enough about that without me throwing in his face again.

Grandma nodded softly, tears falling before reaching a wrinkled hand out for Archer. He took it in his and smiled up at her. "Thank you," she said to Archer. "All of you," she directed at my other mates. "Thank you for keeping her safe and for fixing my mistake."

Then she turned to me. "I am so sorry. I love you, no matter what you've become. You are and always will be my Athena."

I devolved into sobs, sinking in her embrace. We cried together for a few moments longer before pulling back from each other, refreshed, changed… altered.

"When did you last speak to Jacob?" Orpheus asked.

Grandma wiped her eyes with the back of her hand and replied, "I called him right after you called me." She nodded to me.

"What did he say?" Silas chimed in.

"I didn't give him much of a chance to say anything. I was confused and scared, and you just told me that he had you kidnapped, so I was trying to get to the bottom of it all. He just asked if you had called the number I was calling him from, and when I said yes, he hung up," she finished.

"He tracked the call somehow," Samara sighed.

"I kept calling back, but he hasn't answered since then."

"Listen, Grandma, he and his organization are on their way here. They're going to try and kill us," I revealed, and she shook her head, fear plastered on her face. "I need you to get out of town for a few days. I can't focus on what I have to do if I'm worried about you."

She shook her head and began to protest, but I held up a hand.

"Please, don't fight me on this. I need this," I repeated, staring directly into her eyes—a copy of mine and my mother's.

"Okay, honey. I can do that for you. Just please be careful. Promise you'll keep her safe," she said to the others.

"We won't let anyone hurt her. You have our word," Orpheus confirmed.

She threw her arms around my neck and sighed. "I'm so sorry."

"I know."

We held each other for another few precious minutes before I urged her to leave. She insisted on going home to pack a bag, but Orpheus, ever the planner, pulled a wad of cash from his suit jacket– which he somehow had the chance to buy since arriving back in town– and handed it to her, telling her to buy whatever she needed when she was out of town.

Grandma seemed to understand the urgency in his voice because she agreed. We walked her to her car, and I didn't take another breath until her tail lights disappeared safely over the horizon.

I leaned my head on Silas' shoulder and gripped Laz's hand on my other side.

"Are you okay?" Silas asked softly.

I nodded without lifting my head from his shoulder. "I'm glad she's safe." The danger was coming for us, and we had to be ready. For now, though, I let myself enjoy the ocean air, savoring the cool breeze and the sound of the waves crashing against the shore under the moonlight.

I took a long breath of the cool night air and sighed. It was moments like this that I missed my mom the most. When I was scared or afraid, she would always be there for me, keeping me safe and protecting me.

I glanced toward the lighthouse, standing quiet and dark in the moonlight. It was where I had shared my last moments with my mother. The memory tugged at my heart. She had known about vampires. She had only the darkest lies about them at her disposal, yet she still chose not to condemn them.

"I want to go to her grave," I said to my mates, my voice steady.

"Are you sure," Silas asked gently– concern in his voice.

"Yeah, I need to feel her," I admitted, and thankfully nobody else interjected. The light of their support overshadowed the darkness of the past, and I found myself capable of focusing on the good memories with my mother rather than the pain of her loss.

"Would you all like to meet my mom?" I asked softly.

"I'd love to," Samara stated first, reaching for my hand. I smiled gently at her before turning to see the others were nodding.

"Archer?" I asked.

"You want me to come too?" He asked, a little incredulously.

"Of course I do," I replied. He nodded, his eyes glistening with the beginning of unshed tears.

The moon was perched high in the sky, casting a silvery glow over the graveyard as I led my mates and Archer through its quiet, winding paths. The night air was warm but not suffocatingly so, typical of early summer, with a gentle breeze carrying the salty scent of the ocean from the cliffs below. As we walked, the rhythmic sound of waves crashing against the rocks provided a melancholy melody that echoed the phantom beats of my heart.

The graveyard was perched on a cliff overlooking the vast, dark ocean, offering a clear view of the ocean, the town, and the lighthouse. I knew this spot was perfect for her when I first came here. Ancient trees stood fiercely on the outskirts of the cemetery, their branches swaying gently in the night air. Weathered and worn by time, the headstones stood in orderly rows, their inscriptions softened by moss and age. There was a serene beauty to the place, a quiet peace that felt less oppressive than the last time I'd visited.

Approaching my mother's grave, a mix of emotions welled up inside me. Grief, of course, for the loss that still ached like an open wound, but also warmth at the thought of introducing my newfound family to her. My heart constricted tighter with each step, memories of her gentle smile and bright personality flooding back.

We reached her grave, the headstone modest but elegant, etched with her name. *Francessca Landry.* Beneath it, a simple epitaph read: *Beloved Daughter and Mother, Forever in Our Hearts.* I knelt, brushing away a stray leaf that had settled against the stone, and placed my hand on the cool surface, feeling the connection that tied us together even in her absence.

"This is her," I whispered, turning to my mates and Archer. My voice was thick with emotion, but I smiled through it, eager to share this moment. "Mom, these are my mates. Laz, Samara, Silas, and Orpheus." I smiled. "I know, I know. Four partners. I can't believe it either. But it's perfect. They're perfect. I love them." I felt tears slide down my cheeks. "I know you would, too. They are really good to me, Mom. They treat me the way you always told me I deserved to be. I'm really happy." A sob lodged in my throat.

"Hello, Miss Landry. It's an honor to meet you," Laz stated first, stepping forward and placing a hand on the gentle surface of the stone.

"She's one hell of a woman. You should be proud of her," Silas joined in, laying his hand next to Laz's.

"We're lucky to know her," Orpheus added, adding his hands to the stone.

"Thank you for keeping her safe and protecting her. We swear to carry on your legacy," Samara finished, placing her hand next to my mother's name.

"She's also dynamite in bed," Silas teased. Laz and Samara both smacked his chest, sending him stumbling back, clutching his pecs and chuckling. I felt the laugh bubble out of my throat and was instantly thankful to him for lightening the mood.

"And Mom, there's one more person you should meet," I glanced at Archer. He was standing behind us, a few feet away. Nerves clearly wracking through his body as he held his fingers in front of him. "Mom. Meet my brother, Archer."

Archer stepped closer, his expression a blend of reverence and sorrow. He knew he was standing at the resting place of the woman who was so removed from him and yet so intrinsically tied all the same.

"Mom," I continued, my gaze shifting between the headstone and my companions. "This is my family now. They've helped me through so much, and I wish you could have met them. I wish you were here to see how far I've come. How much I've survived because you taught me how to."

The ocean breeze picked up, rustling the grass and whispering through the trees as if the world itself was acknowledging our presence. I let the moment wash over me, feeling a sense of peace knowing I had introduced them to her, even if she wasn't physically there to hear it.

"She would have loved you all," I said, feeling the warmth of my mates and brother around me. "Thank you for coming here with me tonight."

As we stood there, the stars shining above us like distant candles, I felt a profound connection not only to my mother but to those who loved me the way she used to.

ATHENA

FIVE

"Bookworm," Sila's whispered words woke me up late the next day. I didn't even know what time it was anymore, my internal clock shifting into this nocturnal creature. I stretched and yawned, turning my head to see Silas, who lay on his side facing me.

"Good morning," I whispered, smiling sleepily at him. "Or evening, whatever it is." He chuckled.

"You slept all day," he noted, nodding to the clock on the bedside table, which read nine o'clock at night. I stretched.

"I'm like a raccoon," I teased, and Silas laughed with me.

"A very sexy raccoon," he smiled darkly at me.

"Stop it," I said pointedly.

"Stop what?" He asked innocently.

"Stop making eyes with me. I just woke up," I joked, and he leaned forward, pressing a kiss to my lips.

"Get up. I'm taking you somewhere," he said before slipping out from the covers and sliding out of the room. I groaned, yawning once more before tossing the covers off of my body and slipping off the mattress. After washing my face and making myself as presentable as possible, I entered the living room.

My other mates were milling about the room, and all stopped to smile when they saw me. I moved to step toward Samara, who was standing by the coffee machine, but Silas' arms circled my waist and kept me in place. I shot him an inquisitive look, and he shrugged.

"You're mine tonight. I already called it," he said so casually. Laz and Orpheus both rolled their eyes while Samara chuckled.

"I don't even get any coffee?" I whined as he dragged me toward the door.

"Trust me, you won't need any help staying awake," he promised quietly into my ear. His sensual vow sent goosebumps erupting across my skin.

"Make good choices!" Laz called out as we stepped across the threshold into the night air. The sky was not entirely black as night, but the sun that had set several minutes ago left the ghost of a painted sky in its wake. A soft orange glow decorated the horizon, and I was in awe as we ventured across town. Silas held my hand in his, and I only minorly noticed where he was leading me.

It wasn't until we hit the pier that I tore my eyes from the previously painted sky and looked at him.

"Where are we going?" I asked as we traversed the boardwalk and passed the quiet storefronts.

"I made you a promise, baby girl, and I always keep my promises." His eyes sparkled with sinful desires, and my core tightened at his words, but they also brought a memory to the forefront of my mind.

"Speaking of promises, you said something about that guy Orpheus asked for help from…" I prompted, and I heard Silas sigh deeply next to me.

"Elias," he confirmed. I nodded.

"What did you mean by you barely survived the last one?"

He ran a hand through his hair, stopping near a bench and gesturing for me to take a seat. I did and looked up at him as he paced near me.

"Elias deals in promises. They're his currency," he started, and I felt the confusion flood me.

"What does that mean?" I asked.

Silas paused, his eyes distant as if recalling a memory long buried. He paced the ground in front of the bench, the dim light casting soft shadows across his face. He looked almost wistful, but his eyes had an edge of caution.

"Fae don't trade in money or jewels," he explained, and I tried to ignore the shock at hearing the word fae used so casually. "They trade in favors, in promises. When Elias makes a deal, it's bound by magic. Once you agree, you're tied to it until it's fulfilled."

I nodded slowly, processing his words. "And you made a promise to him?"

He sighed, running a hand through his hair, the strands catching the light. "I did. Years ago, when The Wanderers were in a tight spot, we had Nameless right on our heels. It was the closest they'd ever gotten, well, until they captured us. We needed a place to lay low, to hide from the Hunters until we could make a plan and escape. Elias agreed to shield us in his Court, but in return, he wanted a promise."

Silas leaned back, his gaze meeting mine. There was a gravity in his expression, a weight that hadn't been there before. "Could have been any of us to make it, but me, being the brave man I am, stepped up to the plate." he smiled wistfully.

"Brave and humble," I teased, he responded by offering me a smirk. "What did he ask for?" I prompted.

"He wanted me to retrieve some weird ass soul crystal from a place called the Shadow Market. It's not a pleasant place. Really fucking dangerous, honestly. It's almost like the supernatural black market, I guess."

I felt my head spinning at all the new information coming into it.

I frowned, trying to imagine such a place. "What happened?"

"It was worse than I'd imagined," he admitted, his voice dropping to a near whisper. "The Market is full of supernaturals who would kill first, then ask questions later. Elias didn't tell me that this soul crystal wasn't for sale… No, the bastard needed me to steal it. But here's the thing about that place. It's got so much dark magic swirling around that the shadows play tricks on your mind, twisting your perception of reality. It was nearly impossible to keep my focus and find the crystal."

My heart clenched at the thought of him in such peril, and I reached out, placing a hand over his. "But you did it. You kept your promise."

Silas nodded, his gaze softening as he looked at me. "I did. Barely. I found the damn crystal and got the hell out of there. Fulfilled my end of the promise."

"What would have happened if you didn't?"

"Fae can enact whatever punishment they see fit for breaking promises to them, so whatever it would have been, I can guarantee it wouldn't have been pretty."

I squeezed his hand, feeling the strength in his grip. "And that's why you don't want us to get help from him?"

He nodded. "If we accept help from that fae bastard, he will ask for something in return," he said, his voice steady but laced with warning. "And I need you to understand that once you agree, there's no turning back."

"He sounds like a monster," I mused quietly, reaching out for him. Silas grabbed my hand and sat beside me on the bench.

"He's not a monster. Not like the monsters we're used to fighting against, at least. But he is bound by the nature of his kind. He will ask for a promise, and I don't want you to be the one who has to make it."

I nodded, understanding the weight of what he was telling me. "I appreciate the warning, Silas. And I promise I'll be careful."

Silas smiled faintly, a hint of relief in his eyes. "I know you will. Now stop saying that word all willy-nilly, ok?"

I leaned against him, taking comfort in his presence.

"Come on, I have a mate to pleasure," he said with a wink before standing up and offering me a hand. I giggled, reaching for his outstretched hand.

He led me to the bookstore, and with each step, I felt my body tighten with anticipation of what was to come. He slipped a key that I didn't know he had out of his pocket and opened the front door. I raised an eyebrow at him, but he brushed me off with a shrug and pressed a hand to the small of my back to lead me inside.

When I stepped inside, I saw dozens of pink rose petals decorating the floor, unlit candles sitting on the counter, tables, and ground, and only the soft, warm glow of string lights illuminated the space, bathing the store in a sensual light. Silas quickly slipped his lighter from his pocket and lit the candles.

"Didn't want to leave them lit while I grabbed you. You know, fire hazard and all that." I chuckled, but it got caught behind the emotions in my throat. This was such a kind gesture. He always made me feel so special.

Once the last candle was lit, he turned to me, his face even more handsome in the flickering candlelight. He stepped forward, his eyes trailing my body, and I felt my skin blaze under his surveillance.

"I feel a little guilty," I confessed, biting my lower lip.

He tilted his head and narrowed his eyes. "About what, baby girl?" I nearly purred at his sensual nickname for me.

"The Hunters are on their way, we have a whole battle to prepare for, and here I am... being selfish," I admitted, hating how the guilt felt like a weight on my heart.

Silas gripped my chin in his fingers and pulled my eyes up to meet his. He glanced at me with a look so full of love that I almost gasped at the enormity of it. "Our lives are in danger," he whispered. "We are going to have one hell of a fight ahead of us. And there's a chance we aren't the same when all is said and done." He didn't want to say it, but I knew what he meant. Some of us might not make it out alive. "That's a real fucking good excuse to be selfish if ever I heard one."

I sighed.

"No, stop that. Listen to me, Athena." He placed his hands on my shoulders and squeezed gently. "You get to be selfish with us, with me. With love," Silas said, his voice gentle but filled with conviction. He reached out and took my hands in mine, feeling the chill of his skin, the slow pulse of life beneath the surface. His eyes met mine, a storm of emotions swirling within them, and I knew he could see into the pain within me.

"You've had so much taken from you," he continued. "The world hasn't been fair to you, and you've faced hardships that would have broken anyone else. But you're still here, Athena. You're still fighting. You've sacrificed so much for everyone else. It's time you allowed yourself to accept love when it's offered."

I felt a tear slide down my cheek, and he wiped it away with his thumb. "You are allowed to be selfish, Athena. You've earned it with every scar on your heart."

I pressed up onto my tiptoes to kiss him. He slid his arms around my waist and held me there as his mouth devoured mine in a soft, sensual kiss. His lips parted only slightly, giving me just enough room to sweep my tongue inside and brush against his. He moaned and sank into my embrace. When he drew back, I almost protested, but then I saw the devilish look in his eyes, and a shiver of anticipation traveled down my spine.

"Time to make a choice, baby girl," he instructed softly. "I can either make sweet, sensual love to you, make you feel just how special and cherished you are in each kiss, each brush of my skin, or thrust of my cock. I can be gentle and loving."

I choked on air.

"Or I can fuck you like the eager-to-please naughty girl that you are," he admonished in a commanding tone that had me quivering in his hold.

I moaned aloud.

"So, which one will it be?" He asked, pressing a kiss on my collarbone where his serpents rest. I let my head fall back as the bond between us thrummed with eager ecstasy.

"Fuck me," I whispered, leaning forward for a kiss.

"Ah ah ah.." he said, pushing my shoulders back and keeping me from pressing my lips to his. I groaned in frustration. "Use your manners, baby girl."

"Fuck me…" I said again, looking up at him through the curtain of my lashes. "Please, sir," I finished. He groaned deliciously at my words, our own special little phrase. Our own special wicked game. I couldn't wait to play. I loved being with him without any pretense or games, but there was something so appealing about pleasing him this way. It was a game I only ever wanted to play with him.

"You're going to be such a good girl for me, aren't you?" He asked, gripping the back of my neck and forcing my lips to his. I sank into his punishing kiss like butter. My whole body felt heated and warm despite the chilled touch.

"Yes, sir, I am," I swore eagerly. Loving the way I could completely disappear into this place of submission and yet still feel so confident and powerful with him.

"You're going to go to our couch, remove your clothes, and sit there with your legs spread nice and wide for me, and you're going to do it now," he demanded, his eyes alight with lust. I nodded and rushed down the aisles of the bookstores toward the velvet couches. My core was fluttering with eagerness, and I felt my nipples pebble against my shirt. I ripped my shirt over my head and slid my jeans off as fast as possible. I had no idea how close he would be behind me, and I wanted to be ready like he told me to be when he arrived. I was so eager to please him. I felt the urge to be perfect for him in every move I made.

When I was stripped naked, I slid onto the couch and pulled my legs wide. The soft blowing wind from the air conditioner felt nearly sensual against my exposed and eager center. I could feel just how wet I was, but I didn't dare touch myself or relieve the ache because I was a good girl.

I sat there, spread wide and waiting for a few silent minutes. It was torturous as I strained to hear his breathing or any movement from the store. Finally, I heard his footsteps, and my chest heaved as he approached.

"Should we read together again?" He asked from somewhere in the stacks of books. I felt alight all over.

"Yes, sir," I replied.

"Good answer," he breathed quietly, and I licked my bottom lip, trying to distract myself from the ache between my legs. "I'm going to read you a passage, baby girl. And you're not going to move a single inch."

I gasped.

"You're going to be so turned on you can't see straight. Your pussy is going to be soaking wet and begging for relief, but you won't touch yourself. You will not move, do you understand?"

I nodded.

"Words, baby girl. I can't see you, so I need to hear your dirty words," he demanded.

"Yes, sir. I understand." I choked out in my raspy, breathy voice. My arms hooked under my knees and held my legs wide, and I braced myself against the back of the couch, ready for the beautiful torture he was getting ready to inflict.

"'I never wanted anything more in my life than to dip my tongue down and taste her soaking wet pussy.'" He began, and I instantly knew this would be a challenge. "'Her cunt was wet and ready for me to claim as my own, so perfect and tight. Made entirely for me. So, I slid my tongue through her folds, lapping up her arousal like it belonged to me, which it did. She did. She always would.'" I felt my pussy tighten at the dirty words and the images it sent toppling into my mind.

"'Her taste was something so sinful, I knew I'd never be able to forget how it felt on my lips. When I pressed my fingers into her cunt, and her walls tightened around my fingers, I knew she would give me everything I asked her to, and I planned on asking for everything.'"

I was breathing heavily, and my eyes darted around the space, looking for a glimpse of my sinful mate and his watchful eyes.

"'She came on my fingers, her body spasming beneath me as she rode my tongue and fingers to the edge of euphoria. I couldn't wait a moment longer. I needed to be inside of her. I needed her core to squeeze my cock. I slammed into her, her pussy still fluttering with the aftershocks of her orgasm, and then I fucked her.'"

My head fell back against the couch, my eyes falling closed, and I fought against the urge to press my fingers against my more-than-ready pussy.

"'My cock slammed into her over and over and over again. Her breasts bounced against the force, so I had to take the pebbled peak into my mouth. She arched into my mouth, and I couldn't help but circle the clit at the apex of her thighs. That tight bundle of nerves was so eager, so read for my touch that she nearly exploded after just one touch.'" My clit throbbed in almost painful anticipation. I felt my hands wander closer to my core, leaving fiery paths along my thighs on their descent to my pussy.

I just needed a little relief.

I pressed my fingers against my clit, but just as soon as the touch was there, it was snatched away. I opened my eyes to see Silas, now shirtless, standing over me. My offending wrist in one hand and the open book in the other. He glared down at me, disappointment in his gaze.

"You broke the rules, baby girl," he chided. I pouted, hating how defeated I felt.

"I'm sorry, sir, I had to," I replied, trying to sit up, but he kept his hold on me tightly and kept his body positioned between my spread legs so I couldn't close them if I wanted to.

"What should your punishment be?" He mused, his eyes alight with sinful desires.

"I'll do anything," I pleaded.

He thought for a moment, then smirked. He turned the book to me, and I took it in my free hand. He let my wrist go, and I instantly gripped the book to avoid breaking the rules again and reaching for his deliciously exposed body.

"You're going to read for me now, baby girl." I nodded, my eyes drifting to the page and preparing to read, but then he moved and drew my attention back to him. His fingers made quick work of his jeans button, sliding them down his legs and releasing his hard cock from the confinement of his pants. My jaw dropped as I took in the sight of him– the perfect specimen.

"Read, baby girl. And accept your punishment."

I had no idea how this was a punishment, but I barely tore my eyes from his cock and began reading.

"'Her body writhed beneath my punishing thrusts. She slammed down onto my cock as I pressed my body into hers. Her nails tore down my back, and I couldn't contain my hips from pistoning, fucking her like she deserved.'"

I heard his soft moan, and my attention diverted back to him to find him softly stroking his cock, just inches from my soaking wet center. I groaned in near pain. One of my hands reached for him instinctively, but he gripped it with his free hand and returned it to the book.

"Bad girls don't get to touch me," he promised, stroking his length sensually.

"Silas," I whined.

"Read, baby girl. Accept your punishment, and then if you're good, I'll fuck you," he vowed, and the promise was almost too exciting a proposition. So I pulled my gaze from his stiff and eager length and continued reading.

"'She was going to come, and I was going to feel every inch of her fall apart beneath me. The way she fell into an orgasm was so sexy. Her core tightened around my cock, squeezing me until I could feel my balls tighten and my climax rise. Her back arched, and her mouth fell open as she screamed my name. I pounded into her as her orgasm beckoned my own.'" I heard him moan, and the sinful sounds of his hand sliding along his cock was almost enough to draw my eyes away again, but I didn't dare. I wanted my reward. "'I emptied myself into her, her core taking all of me the way she was designed to. Her body was mine, and I was hers.'" I finished in a breathy whisper.

I closed the book and looked up at Silas, who had slowed his strokes and was staring down at me sinfully.

"That's my good girl," he praised, and I preened under the adoration. "You need me, don't you?" He asked, his eyes looking down at my glistening pussy.

"Yes, sir," I begged.

"Say it," he said, leaning forward slightly, bringing the tip of his cock to just about an inch away from making contact with my swollen clit. I threw my head back and fought against the urge to push my hips up to meet him.

"I need your cock, sir. Please," I cried out.

The first press of his head against my clit was like a bomb detonating. I cried out his name but kept my body still. He slid the tip along my pussy lips gently, teasingly. Never quite pushing in. The sensation was almost too much.

"Oh my god, baby girl. You are so wet," he said, dropping the facade of my dominant sir just slightly. "I could just slide in if I wanted to."

"Only for you," I promised, earning me a hum of approval. I felt my body tingle with pride.

"I am going to fuck this pussy like you've never been fucked before," he swore, his eyes turning feral. The red tint shone through.

"I dare you," I challenged.

His eyes flashed darkly, and he smirked, pressing the tip of his cock against my clit again, and I arched into it. "Oh, is that so?" He asked, sliding his cock down my pussy toward the entrance and pressing in just enough for me to feel the slight stretch but not enough to satisfy my wanton need. "You dare me?" He asked teasingly.

"Please, Silas," I begged, but he pulled back, leaving me pussy empty and eager.

"Let's get one thing straight, baby girl," he said just as he pressed his cock against my entrance again, pressing forward a little more than last time, but still not nearly enough before pulling back again. I sighed frustratingly. "You do not get to challenge me when we play our little games," he said, sliding his cock up and down my pussy lips coating it in my arousal. My lips fell open on a gasp. "Tell me you understand."

"I understand," I replied with a moan.

He slid his cock down until it pressed against my ass ever so slightly before sliding back up my soaked folds.

"You are mine to play with, mine to command, mine to fuck," he said, the look in his eyes so feral and ferocious I almost growled in response. The nearly animalistic side of me fighting for dominance.

"I need you, Silas. Please, sir. Fuck me like you own me," I begged.

Then he slammed his hips forward and sheathed his cock so deep into my aching pussy that I let out a guttural scream. The sound was almost inhuman as pleasure erupted through my body. I was so tightly wound that the first orgasm ripped through me unexpectedly and wracked through my body.

"Yes, that's it, baby girl, grip my cock as you come," Silas demanded as he slammed into me over and over again. His words were broken and strained as he fought against his building climax.

He slammed into me, making good on his promise to fuck me like an eager-to-please naughty girl. I so rarely let myself let go the way I did when we played this game. It was so freeing and so dirty.

His cocked slammed into me, and I was falling apart all over again as he claimed my body as his. His mouth closed over one of my nipples, and I arched into his hold. My body felt worshipped, every nerve ending wholly wound up and tingling under his expert touch.

"I'm in love with you," I called out, an exclamation in the heat of the moment. His eyes softened, the dominant 'sir' slipping away to reveal my Silas.

"Fuck, I'm in love with you too, bookworm," he swore gently before slamming his hips against mine again and stealing my breath. His fingers found my clit and pressed deliciously sinful circles against it until my stomach muscles were clenching, and I was climaxing all over again. He leaned over me, bracing himself on the back of the couch as he came too, his body jerking violently as his orgasm wracked through him. We sat in silence for a few moments, his cock remaining idly inside of me as our breathing slowed and our bodies stopped trembling.

"I don't want you to leave," I whined, locking my ankles around his back and holding him to my body. He smiled down at me.

"I'm not going anywhere, baby." He picked me up, keeping me pressed against him so that his cock would remain pressed inside of me. He was sitting down on the couch, leaning back so that he was horizontal, and I was straddling his body. I leaned forward, pressing my cheek against his chest, and counted his heartbeats for a long while.

"I love playing that game with you," I whispered sheepishly, suddenly more self-conscious about my submissive state.

"So do I," he promised, tracing lines down my spine with his fingertips.

"I never thought I'd ever be able to be vulnerable like that with someone ever again," I admitted quietly, avoiding eye contact.

"After.." he started, and I nodded.

"Yeah," I finished for him. "I used to wake up in the middle of the night and feel his hands on my body. Like imprints." I shuddered. "I never felt so weak, so submissive. All I could do was lay there and let it happen. I couldn't fight back." His arms closed around my body, holding me tightly to his chest.

"I hate that I didn't find you early enough to save you from him," Silas said, seething beneath me.

"You are saving me, all of you, every single day," I sat up a little, just enough to look into his eyes. "With everything you say and do, you're all saving me from the pain of those memories. Orpheus makes me feel like I have agency again and can ask for what I need. Samara makes me feel like I can be sensitive again and let people in. Laz shows me that my scars can be stories and that I'm stronger because of them. And you… You give me the freedom to let go, to trust someone again, the way I haven't been able to since he took what he did from me."

Silas ran a hand along my face, tucking a lock of hair behind my ear.

"You saved my life, Silas," I swore and kissed his lips. He drank my kiss delicately, sensually, savoring every moment of it. I felt his cock twitch to life within my core.

"I'm going to make love to you now, Athena," he promised against my lips.

"I dare you," I challenged with a wink, rolling my hips tauntingly.

*

When Silas and I had had our delicious fill of each other and arrived back at the house, I was sated and happy. Silas kept an arm around my shoulders and led me to the kitchen island, where my other mates gathered around a Shockgrove map. We sat hunched around the kitchen island, the air thick with tension as we discussed our plans. The room was dimly lit, the soft glow of the overhead lights casting warm shadows on the walls. Despite the relatively calm atmosphere, I could feel the undercurrent of urgency in our conversations as we strategized our defenses against whatever might come next. Every day we sat here strategizing was another day closer to the Hunter's inevitable attack. I could feel that, and so could everyone else.

Laz was leaning against the counter, and their brow furrowed as they jotted down notes on a pad, their gaze flicking up to meet mine with a reassuring smile. Samara sat beside me, her fingers tapping rhythmically on the countertop, deep in thought. Silas and Orpheus were across from us, engaged in a quiet discussion, their voices low and focused.

"We need to make sure we're ready for anything," Orpheus said, his voice steady but determined.

Silas joined in. "They won't stop coming, and we can't afford to be caught off guard."

Samara nodded, her eyes reflecting the same determination. "We could call the covens in Maine to set up defensive wards, maybe?"

"If you think they'd use their magic to protect vampires, you will be sorely disappointed," Silas chuffed.

"Covens? Like witches?" I gasped.

"It's a big world, bookworm," Silas added, tossing me a sly smirk. My head felt like it was spinning.

"We can't ask them, but we do have other potential reinforcements coming," Orpheus promised.

Just as Silas was about to respond, the kitchen door swung open, and Archer rushed in. I flinched instantly, a reflex now due to my painful reaction to the sun's rays, but luckily, no sun spilled through the doorway. It was well into the evening, nearly midnight. Time had gotten away from me. We were all startled, not having heard his approach– a testament to the stealth he'd honed through years of Hunter training. I relaxed the moment he locked eyes with me, but he didn't. His presence was charged with a panicked intensity. His eyes were wide with anger and panic, and his usually calm demeanor rattled. I heard his heart rate racing, pumping his blood through his veins.

"We need to go to the lighthouse," he said, his voice urgent. "Right now."

The suddenness of his entrance and the tension in his words shocked us. Silas and Orpheus exchanged a quick glance, their expressions shifting from curiosity to concern.

"What's going on?" Orpheus asked, his voice calm but wary as he approached my brother.

"They left a message," Archer replied, the words heavy.

A chill ran through me at his tone, a sense of foreboding settling in my gut. I met Archer's gaze, seeing the worry etched in his features. Whatever message had been left, it was enough to shake him.

Without hesitation, we moved as one, gathering what we needed and following Archer out the door. The night air was cool against my skin as we hurried to the lighthouse, a sense of urgency propelling us forward.

The walk was silent, each of our heads on a swivel, the gravity of the situation pressing down on us. As we approached the lighthouse, its silhouette stark against the night sky, I felt a mix of dread and determination.

As we reached the entrance, Archer paused, his eyes scanning the surroundings before he turned to us. "Be ready," he said, his voice low but persistent. "We don't know what we're walking into."

We paused at the base of the base of the lighthouse, and I breathed in deeply, letting the scent of salt and seaweed fill my lungs. This place, which meant so much to me and carried so much love and so much pain, was once a place I called our spot but had been tainted. I could almost hear my mother's laughter in the wind and feel her presence beside me. The nights I spent here with her flooded my mind. I remembered how we came here and sat at the peak, talking for hours as the waves crashed around us. She always made me feel safe, even when the world seemed to be falling apart. Her smile, gentle touch, how she would brush a stray lock of hair behind my ear or tell me everything would be okay. All those little things that made her my mother. Standing here now, I felt her spirit wrapping around me like a comforting embrace, preparing me for what was next.

Silas' voice broke through my thoughts. "Shit."

"What is it?" Laz asked.

"See for yourself," he said, pointing to the side of the old beacon. We shifted to his position to see what he was referring to. My heart sank as I took in the ominous symbol. Two offset triangles and a stake. Two words painted in bright red paint dripped like crimson blood down the side of the lighthouse.

Nisi Nox.

It was only my whispered words that cut through the emptiness of the chilly night air.

"They're here."

SAMARA

SIX

I felt their presence the moment they arrived. Turning over my shoulder away from the Nameless mark, I saw them approach. Nameless was here. Fear gripped me, a cold, unyielding terror that had the potential to paralyze me. But I couldn't afford to be scared. We needed to fight for Athena, for our survival…for Alora. My gaze darted around, taking in the faces of my mates and Archer, all of whom wore determined expressions despite the fear flickering in their eyes.

I scanned the Hunter's ranks, counting quickly. At least sixty. Shit. Then I saw her. Athena's best friend, Davia, was held tightly in a wicked embrace by one of the Hunters, her face pale with fear as she cried out and fought against their hold. A surge of anger and protectiveness shot through me, but it was Athena's reaction that nearly broke me. Her eyes blazed with fury, and she stepped forward, ready to charge and rescue Davia.

"Athena, no!" I grabbed her arm, pulling her back. "That's what they want."

She stopped, her chest heaving with rage and desperation, her eyes red and fangs viciously bared, but she knew I was right. Charging in blindly would only get us all killed. We needed a plan, and we needed it now. I sent my power out toward Davia, shocked to find that it was not only powerful enough to reach her at this distance but enough to heal the pain in her arms from where the Hunters had roughly grabbed her.

Finally, my eyes landed on Jacob Bennett. His eyes were wild, and his face was twisted in almost wicked determination. Alora's face flashed in my mind. There was a time when I wanted his death more than I wanted anything. But now I had Athena, and for some cruel reason, he was her father. I'd kill him for her, but I'd also spare him for her if she asked me to.

"Up the steps," Archer hissed, already moving toward the lighthouse.

We retreated up the winding staircase, the narrow space offering a temporary reprieve from the overwhelming numbers below. Each step echoed with the sound of our hurried ascent, the weight of the situation pressing heavily on us.

At the top, we paused, trying to catch our breath and form a strategy. I could feel the panic rising again, but I forced it down. This was no time to lose control.

"Athena," I whispered, turning to her. "We need to think. We can't save Davia if we're dead.

She nodded, though her eyes remained fixed on the direction of her best friend below as the Hunters continued to surround the lighthouse. Her hands clenched into fists, the frustration palpable. "We need a distraction," she said, her voice tight. "Something to draw them away from Davia."

Orpheus nodded. "I'll go. I'm fast enough to lead them on a chase."

"No," Laz interjected. "We stay together. We can use the lighthouse to our advantage. Force them to come to us one by one." I glanced around, seeing the agreement in everyone's eyes. It was risky, but it was our best shot. We couldn't afford to let fear dictate our actions.

The moment the Hunters started up the lighthouse stairs, the atmosphere shifted. I felt it. We all did. The clanging of their boots echoed up the spiral staircase, each step sending a jolt of tension through my body. I steeled myself, knowing my role in this battle was to heal and keep us all alive.

Orpheus and Silas were the first line of defense.

As the first wave of Hunters breached the top of the stairs, the two of them dispatched them quickly and precisely. They fought side by side, a perfect blend of brute strength and lethal grace. Orpheus's sharpened nails flashed in the dim light while Silas's raw power sent them flying back down the stairs, knocking down approaching Hunters behind them.

A sudden clatter caught my attention, and I turned to see Laz on the deck, a bucket of rainwater in their hands. Their eyes glinted with determination as they stared at the liquid within the vessel. They offered me a hopeful shrug, then pushed past Silas and Orpheus to pour the bucket's contents down the stairs. The liquid splashed onto the Hunters below. Screams filled the air as the acid burned their faces and hands, rendering some lifeless and sending the others stumbling back in agony.

Despite the chaos, I kept my focus on healing. Whenever one of them took a hit, I was there, my hands burning with healing energy. Cuts closed, bruises faded, and the pain in their eyes dimmed as I focused my energy on them.

Eventually, the Hunters regained composure and continued their assault. Silas and Oprhues held the line as best they could, but a few slipped past, rushing toward Laz, Athena, and me.

Athena was initially distracted by the sight of Davia below, but as the Hunters flooded the area, she finally joined the fray. This was her first time fully utilizing her vampiric abilities in a fight, and she took to it with a natural adeptness that was both awe-inspiring and terrifying. My dead heart thumped viciously with fear and worry for her. She seemed to be holding her own quite well, evading their attacks. If I weren't so afraid of losing her, I'd be proud.

"Athena, behind you!" I shouted, seeing a Hunter sneaking up on her. She spun around, catching his arm mid-swing and twisting it with a sickening crunch. With a swift kick, she sent him tumbling down the stairs, adding to the growing pile of bodies below.

Orpheus and Silas kept the line, their coordinated attacks keeping the Hunters at bay. Laz, having emptied the bucket, joined the fight with elongated fangs desperate to sink into the Hunters' flesh.

Despite the overwhelming odds, we fought with everything we had and held our own against the constant onslaught Nameless.

But the battle was far from over. More Hunters kept coming, their determination and anger unwavering and relentless. I moved between my coven, healing wounds as they happened, and they kept happening. We were outnumbered.

"There's too many of them!" Laz cried out as several more Hunters spilled out from the staircase and began attacking. Silas screamed as a poisoned blade sliced across his torso. Athena's eyes snapped toward the sound, and distracted, she took an arrow to the chest. She writhed in pain. I sent my magic out toward both of them, desperate to keep them safe, when a flying fist knocked me back.

I hit the ground and groaned at the pain that was radiating through me at that moment. The Hunter who had managed to hit me stood above me, a wooden stake poised to slam into my chest. I threw my legs up, slamming my feet against his chest, and sent him flying back, toppling into another Hunter, which gave Orpheus the advantage he needed to rip their throats out.

"Athena, Archer," a familiar, eerie voice called from the base of the lighthouse. The Hunters stilled at the command of their leader.

I shook with fury. How dare he say her name. How dare he speak to her.

"Come down here and join us. We don't want to harm humans," Jacob bellowed from the ground below. The Hunters at the staircase ceased, paused in a tense standoff with Silas and Orpheus as they awaited the result of his offer.

Athena and Archer shared a brief look at each other, their faces and clothing covered with the blood of their father's Hunters, before walking toward the ledge of the deck. They leaned against the railing and looked down at the man below.

I took this brief respite to soothe my coven's injuries. The wound on Athena's chest where the arrow had pierced was deep, and there was a toxin there that seemed to come from the arrow before she had removed it. I focused all my energy on that wound, banishing the toxin from her blood and healing her. She visibly relaxed when I finished.

Silas' chest was the worst of our injuries. It bled profusely because of the anticoagulant that the blade was laced with. I had to focus intensely on that one to ensure he was healed. It would take more than I could give now, but he was at least upright and breathing.

The others had minor cuts and bruises that I worked on as Athena, and Archer glanced down at their father. This fight was far from over, but if I had anything to say about it, we'd all make it out of here alive. Bennett would never take another person I loved from me.

ARCHER

SEVEN

"You are fighting for the wrong side," my father called out to us from his place on the ground. My teeth ground against each other, and my jaw tightened as my eyes saw that his arm was now barred across Davia's throat. She looked so scared, so afraid, and all I wanted to do was protect her. Get her as far away from all this as possible. She didn't deserve to suffer at the hands of my father.

"Let her go!" Athena seethed.

"I will, when you both come down here, where you belong," he claimed. I rolled my eyes.

"I don't belong anywhere with you, asshole," she replied, pure pain in her voice.

"Archer, you know better than this. You cannot seriously want to fight for those monsters… to die for them?" He spat, nothing but vitriolic hate in his tone.

"I'd rather die for them than believe another second of your lies," I growled back.

"You won't win this fight, don't be on the losing side," he pleaded, and to his credit, behind the hateful rhetoric, he did sound like a concerned father.

"Why won't you consider that you're wrong?" I begged, desperate for the man I once called my father to replace this vicious villain before me.

"Because those creatures are evil, and they deserve to rot in hell like the abominations they are!" His arm tightened around Davia's throat, and she cried out.

"Let her go right now, or I will make you," I threatened, my hands gripping the railing so tightly that I was nervous that I may actually break it.

"My mother was right about you," Athena blurted, even-toned and angry. My father's face paled.

"Your mother doesn't understand," he argued.

"Are you willing to kill your son to prove this point to yourself? Are you?" I howled. He shook his head but didn't vocalize a response.

"What about me, dad?" Athena cried, and everyone took a collective inhale as the word spilled from her tongue. "What about me? Would you kill me? Would you kill me after leaving us to feed your stupid obsession?" She screamed, and his face dropped.

"Athena.. I.." He stuttered.

"Answer me!" She sobbed.

"You don't understand," he pleaded wild anger in his eyes. I eyed the point of contact where his arm pressed against Davia. I wouldn't let him hurt her. I'd jump off this damn tower to stop it if I had to.

His face twisted into an almost unrecognizable mask of fury. I had always feared him and sought his approval, but now I saw him for what he truly was— a man consumed by his own darkness.

"Dad, let her go! And just leave. We are no threat to you." I shouted, my voice echoing against the cliffs. The ocean roared below, a fitting backdrop to the chaos unfolding around us.

He shook his head, tightening his grip on Davia. "You don't understand, Archer. This is for your own good. For all of us. I'm protecting humankind."

Anger and sorrow twisted inside me, but I couldn't let it consume me. I had to stay focused. "This isn't the way. Let her go, and we can talk."

He sneered. "Talk? If you two won't join me, then there's nothing left to say."

Before I could react, the Hunters surged forward, attacking with renewed ferocity at my father's twisted command. Their numbers seemed endless, and despite our best efforts, we were overpowered. I fought alongside my sister and her mates as Hunter after Hunter arrived up the staircase at a rate even we couldn't keep up with. Blood and sweat mingled, and the weight of each strike grew heavier.

A Hunter that I remembered from headquarters broke through our defenses, slashing at Silas with a serrated blade. He grunted in pain, stumbling back into Orpheus. While they were distracted, another Hunter struck out against them with a garlic-laced whip. It struck Orpheus across the face, leaving a blistering red line. He winced. Athena called out for her mates, which only made her more of a target. The Hunter to her left reached out and got their hands around her neck, squeezing as she fought against them. Laz and I jumped to assist her, but another Hunter pulled me back. He landed a blow across my face, and the sickening crunch echoed through the night air as my nose broke. Samara was healing us as fast as she could, but the injuries were coming too quickly.

We were losing. The realization hit me like a punch to the gut, much more painful than the one I had just sustained to my face. We couldn't hold out much longer.

We were going to lose.

A bright flash of light erupted from the broken light beside us. Bright, gold, shimmering light spilled into the space, cutting through the night sky like a blade. Fighting ceased as Wanderer and Hunter alike shielded their eyes from the assaulting light.

When the golden pool of light began to dissipate, my eyes adjusted to the scene around me. Similar, and yet somehow completely different. There was another figure on the deck of the lighthouse now, tall and slender with shaggy black hair flowing like a river of midnight, wearing almost regal attire and a circlet of ivy. His eyes glowed with an ethereal golden light as he gracefully moved through the remaining Hunters in the tower. With a flick of his wrist, he sent daggers of what looked like shimmering light speeding toward them, their weapons clattering uselessly to the ground.

On the ground below, a second figure– buff and imposing with dark skin and shaggy hair pulled back at the nap of his neck- charged into the fray. He swung a massive sword with effortless strength, holding back the Hunters, who remained on the ground with ease.

A third figure, a red-headed warrior with fierce determination in his glowing eyes, appeared beside my father and Davia. With a quick, precise motion, he disarmed my father, pulling Davia away from his grasp. My father's eyes widened in shock as the red-headed stranger slammed a shimmering fist against his temple, knocking him flat out.

The regal one near us flourished his hand, and an icy chill emanated from his magic. The air around him shimmered with energy, a palpable force that made the hair on the back of my neck stand on end. A surge of energy erupted from him, spreading out in a wave that washed over the battlefield. The Hunters froze in place, their weapons mid-swing, their expressions locked in various states of shock and anger. I blinked, trying to comprehend what had just happened. The Hunters were suspended in mid-motion as if time itself had stopped for them.

I glanced over the railing to find he had also affected the Hunters on the ground.

"Elias," Orpheus panted, offering a hand for the stranger. "I see you got my message."

The tall man, Elias, took Orpheus' arm and held it. "Just in time, it would seem." Orpheus shrugged, pain coloring his expression.

Uninterested in the welcome party, I sprinted down the steps, desperate to see if Davia was safe. Weaving carefully through the frozen Hunters that littered the steps, I heard the others follow behind me, but I didn't turn to look. I had to get to her. I had to see her.

Spilling out of the lighthouse onto the clearing, I immediately saw the two additional strangers, each gripping one of my father's arms as he hung limp and knocked out in their hold. They eyed me curiously as I sprinted toward Davia.

I stopped just short of pulling her into my arms, looking her over for any injuries. "Davia, are you okay?" I gasped.

Her eyes met mine. I could see that she had been crying. Her blue eyes were bright and mesmerizing. She was just as captivating as she had been the first time I saw her. She opened her mouth, and I thought she was going to say something to me, but instead, her palm struck against my cheek, sending me reeling back from her slap. The sting in my cheek was vicious. I cupped my cheek with a hand and glanced back at her.

"That's for kidnapping Athena," she said, and I didn't have any time to react before her knee came up into my solar plexus and sent me toppling to the ground on all fours with a grunt. She leaned down so that her lips were by my ear. "And that's for lying to me about it."

"Davia!" Athena's voice called from behind me. Davia stood and rushed forward to embrace her friend. I felt the warm caress of Samara's healing against my stinging cheek and aching stomach. I sent her a thankful nod, and she smiled softly at me.

I stood and turned to watch Davia and Athena cry into each other's arms. I smiled, appreciating for a moment how fiercely these two protected each other. It was the kind of relationship I had never really had with anyone, but I was definitely starting to feel for my sister—and her mates, too, I guess, which was a wild turn of events.

"Thank you for your help…" Athena directed to the strangers who had arrived in the light. I took this moment of relative peace to really study the newcomers who had saved the day. The regal-looking one that Orpheus had called Elias was pale. His sharp cheekbones and attire reminded me of portraits of royalty I might find in a history textbook. The redhead who held one of my father's arms had cropped hair just above his ears and wore much more modern attire than the others. Sporting dark wash jeans and a Henley. The buff one, who looked like a gladiator, wore what could only be described as a suit of armor you'd see at a Renaissance faire.

They were a mess of genre that frankly had me even more confused now that I got a closer look.

"Elias," he offered. "And this is Ronan," he indicated to the red-head. "And Jasper." The tank of a man grunted his acknowledgment. "Two of the most trusted members of my Court."

"Court?" I asked, eyeing them.

"You don't know who we are?" Ronan chimed in, his voice like molten lava with how much disdain was laced in the tone.

"He's not a vamp, Ronan," Samara replied. "And she's a fresh-turn."

Ronan nodded, and Elias stepped forward to Davia, gripping her hand and pressing a kiss against her knuckles, making my blood boil. "And you? What is your relationship to the supernatural?"

She stood her ground against him, seemingly unaffected by his imposing nature, as she ripped her hand back. "I'm a human, and you are in my space, so I kindly ask you to back the fuck up."

I heard Orpheus and Silas inhale sharply at that, bracing themselves for retaliation. I prepared myself to jump in if it seemed like she needed it. But instead, a smile spread across his lips, and he laughed darkly.

"We appreciate your help, Elias," Laz chimed in, trying to pull his attention away.

"Well, you're not quite out of the woods yet." He indicated to the frozen Hunters who were poised to attack. I wondered how long he could hold them in their place. "We are always willing to make a deal. Orpheus knows that," Elias answered, smiling coyly at him before glancing back at Davia.

"Alright then, get on with it. What do you want?" Silas challenged.

Elias tore his eyes from Davia and smiled at Silas. The almost diplomatic way he surveyed him sent chills down my spine.

"Tsk tsk tsk, is that any way to thank your backup?" Elias asked tauntingly. "I don't have to assist. Would you prefer to handle them on your own?"

"You have our gratitude, and you will have your promise, whatever it is. Name it," Orpheus declared, sending a look of warning to Silas, who huffed but nodded. I sensed a story there, but now wasn't the time to dive into it.

Elias shared a look with Ronan and Jasper, a silent exchange. Jasper nodded to Elias rather quickly, without much fuss. He seemed the quiet type. Ronan, however, looked pissed, anger burning in his eyes, but eventually he nodded too. Now having whatever confirmation he needed, Elias turned back to the group.

"Well, in exchange for helping you with your little Hunter problem, as you are aware from the last time you asked me for my assistance, the price remains a single promise."

"Oh yeah, we remember," Silas quipped under his breath.

"Name it," Orpheus said, ignoring Silas, and something about the way Elias smiled had my stomach dropping.

"I want this one to promise to spend an entire year with me at my Court," he said, pointing at Davia.

"Not a chance," I said at the same time as Athena called out, "No way!" Davia's eyes widened, and she took a step back. I moved a step closer, trying to put myself between her and the royal asshat.

"I said you'd have a promise from me," Orpheus argued, trying to calm the chaos for the moment.

"No, you said I'd have my promise. Whatever I want. I believe you said. Name it," he taunted darkly. I felt my fists clench at my side as fury built up in my chest.

Orpheus cursed under his breath.

"You should know to be careful with your words by now, my dear friend," Elias said.

"She's not going anywhere with you," I demanded.

"See, that's not how this works, love. If you want us to do as you ask, I need my payment." Elias titled his head, offering me a condescending look.

"Fuck you," Athena spat. His eyes lit up with glee at the challenge in her tone. He stepped forward, tenting his fingers in front of him.

"I understand. If you don't want to make the promise, we can always leave…" He lifted his hands, wiggling his finger. I saw the Hunters begin to twitch, their movement returning to them in tiny increments.

"Elias…please," Samara begged, eyeing the pack of Hunters around us. She knew as I did that we weren't guaranteed a win if left to our own devices.

"The promise is all it will take," Elias confirmed.

"There has to be something else you want," Orpheus urged eagerly.

"Afraid not. My terms have been set," he replied flippantly. My heart rate sped, fury boiling just beneath the surface.

"That's not fair!" Athena cried out.

"It seems we are unable to come to an agreement on this. We shall take our leave now," Elias said smugly, lifting his hand as the Hunters' reanimation sped up. Any second now, they would be back to attacking, and we would be outnumbered. I braced myself for the second round.

"Wait," Davia called out. All our heads turned to face her. "I'll do it."

"What?" I exclaimed.

"Davia, no…" Athena challenged. Davia placed a hand on Athena's cheek and nodded fiercely.

"I can't lose you again, Athena," she blurted before taking a deep breath and closing her eyes. "I was so scared. You're my best friend, my sister, and I thought you were…" she cried softly, tears stained her cheeks. "I brought Louis and Greg into your life. I did that. I'm the reason they hurt you."

Athena started to protest, but Davia shook her head. "No, don't try to take this guilt away. If doing this saves your life, then it is the easiest decision I will ever make."

Athena was crying, her shoulders wracking with sobs.

"Besides, you know I've always wanted to take a year off to travel," Davia added with a chuckle. They embraced, and I saw Athena nod softly.

"Are you sure?" Athena whispered. My chest tightened… No, she wasn't going to actually do it, was she?

"Let me do this for you," Davia pleaded.

"Thank you, Davia," Athena confessed, and I stepped forward involuntarily.

"No, not a chance. You are not going with these strangers, Davia. We know nothing about them. What if they hurt you?" I was fuming.

Davia turned to glare at me. "Not all strangers are like you, Archer."

It stung, but I deserved it.

"You can't go…"

"It's not your choice to make," she retorted.

"Then I'm going with you," I blurted out, and shock colored her expression.

"What?" Davia asked just as Athena stepped forward and gripped my arm.

"Archer…" Athena started.

"Just to keep an eye on you, make sure you're safe," I justified. I still was not even sure what I was saying, I only knew that I needed to do this.

"I don't need your help," Davia argued, but I saw it. The slight twinge of relief in her features eclipsed the fear behind her mask of strength and indifference for the briefest moments. She was afraid and needed me, even if she wouldn't admit it.

"I know, but I'm offering it anyway. Please, let me go to be there for you if you need me." I met her eyes, and a silent understanding passed between us before she nodded.

"So, do we have a promise?" Elias prompted. I turned to see the look on his face, and he seemed almost hopeful.

Davia gripped Athena's hand and smiled, turning her icy glare to the figure before her. "Archer and I will join you in your Court for one year." She didn't meet my gaze, but my heart lept at the trust she placed in me.

"Say it," Elias commanded darkly, holding his hand out for Davia. She placed her palm in his. He then turned to me and held his other hand out for me to take. I held his eyes as I did.

"I promise." We both said in unison.

A small crack of thunder erupted from where our hands were joined, and a bright golden light danced around our arms. I shielded my eyes until the light began to dissipate. In its place was a faint golden vine of ivy climbing up her forearm, and when I looked, I wore a matching mark on my skin. Elias smiled down at his arms, which also bore the mark of our promise.

I felt changed. Different. I knew that what we promised would change everything, and there was no going back from it now. At least she wasn't in it alone.

"Great," Elias said, giddy happiness on his features. "Shall we finish off your Hunter problem then?" He directed to Orpheus, who looked lost.

"Yes," he answered, shaking his head.

Elias nodded to the others, Jasper and Ronan, who set my father's body down on the ground and moved to stand before the Hunters, who were still frozen.

"Are you going to kill them like that?" Laz asked.

"Where's the fun in that?" Ronan answered with a wicked smile just as Elias dropped the magic holding the Hunters. The battlefield once again erupted into chaos, but this time, we had the advantage.

Elias stood at the center of the fray, his hands glowing with mysterious energy. With a flick of his wrist, he sent magic bolts crashing into the Hunters, knocking them back and creating barriers to protect us from the Hunter's onslaught.

Jasper, the towering figure of strength, easily tore through the Hunters in front of him. His shaggy brown hair whipped around as he swung a massive sword, cleaving through enemies like they were nothing more than paper. I suddenly found myself incredibly grateful he was on our side. Ronan, the red-headed warrior, moved with a supernatural stealth. He slipped through the shadows, striking with deadly precision. One moment, he was there. The next, he was gone, leaving a trail of incapacitated Hunters in his wake.

Silas and Orpheus joined the fray with a savage fury. Their fangs bared as they let the pain and anger of all the years that Nameless hunted them fuel their strikes. They moved like predators, their vampire instincts making them formidable, but their fury making them unstoppable.

My eye caught on Laz as they ran toward the cliff's edge, pursued by several Hunters. Panic gripped me as they approached the ledge, but just as they reached it, they spun on their heel to face their assailants. Their features were more vampire than human as they focused on the mist from the crashing waves that spilled around them. The water from the wave rained down on the Hunters who had chased Laz, and the moment the liquid hit their skin, they screamed and clutched their burning faces. The smell of burning flesh filled the air, and I tried not to look at their melting skin and instead focus on the Hunters ahead.

Samara stood back, trying to keep each of us healed and in the fight while Athena moved with deadly precision, her movements a blur as she took on a Hunter. With a swift, clean motion, she knocked him out, her eyes cold and determined. She had fully embraced her new vampiric strengths, and it showed in the way she fought. I thought maybe I'd be afraid to see her like this. But she was powerful, and I felt the kind of pride that could only ever be reserved for her—my sister.

And then there was me. My sole focus was protecting Davia. She clung to my side, accepting my help without hesitation. Utilizing my training, I managed to fight off any Hunter who came too close. Her trust in me gave me the strength to keep going.

As the last of the Hunters fell, a heavy silence settled over the bloodstained battlefield. We stood together, breathing heavily but victorious. The immediate threat was gone, and we had a moment to catch our breath for the first time in what felt like forever.

Elias lowered his hands, the glow fading as he looked around at the aftermath. Jasper and Ronan stood tall, their expressions a mix of relief and exhaustion, while Silas and Orpheus wiped the blood from their fangs, their eyes searching for Athena. Laz stepped away from the cliff and stood near Samara, who healed their skin from the burns they sustained from their acidic waves. Athena, her fingers still dripping with blood, smiled softly at her mates.

I turned to Davia, who looked at me with wide eyes. "Are you okay?" I asked, my voice rough with worry.

"Yeah, I'm fine," she answered, and I almost believed her. She rushed over and hugged Athena, and the two of them devolved into exhausted laughter.

"Thank you, Elias," Orpheus said, stepping toward him. Elias bowed his head in acknowledgment before turning to face Davia.

"Take your time. Get your affairs in order," he spoke calmly as if he hadn't just been in the heat of a wicked battle. He pulled a card from his pocket and held it out for her. She took it, and the shake in her hands was almost imperceptible. But I saw it. "Meet us here when you're ready."

She nodded her silent agreement.

"What are we supposed to do about them," Athena whispered, her eyes wide as she took in the bloody mess surrounding us. There were bodies littered across the grass and spilling into the lighthouse. Bright red blood darkened the grass at our feet. It was a horrific sight.

"I'm not sure," Orpheus admitted, and I could tell that he hated not having the answers. Anal retentive bastard.

Elias waved his hand before him, sending a rippling wave of magic out across the field. The bodies dotting the space slowly disappeared behind the shimmering veil of his magic. The blood spilled along the ground sank into the earth, leaving no trace of the battle that had occurred here or the death that remained.

"Consider that one a freebie." Elias winked as he looked over his shoulder at Ronan and Jasper, who stepped forward to flank him. "Until next time." The bright light that heralded their arrival erupted again, and I once again found myself shielding my eyes. What the hell was it with those assholes and bright lights?

Athena was wrapped in the embrace of her mates, sharing an intimate moment of relief, so I averted my eyes to give them their privacy and walked over to my unconscious father, crouching down to see him clearly. He was sprawled on the grass. His face looked almost peaceful, which felt like such an oxymoron. He was a vicious man, a violent creature who wanted death and destruction.

He was also my father.

"You didn't have to do that," Davia whispered as she approached. I kept my eyes trained on my father's face but shook my head.

"Yes, I did," I admitted.

"This doesn't make up for what you did," she said. I stood but didn't turn to face her.

"I know."

We stood silently, avoiding each other's eyes for a few prolonged moments until Athena joined us.

"What are we going to do about him?" She asked softly. I shrugged.

"I don't know," I replied. We could kill him and ensure that he would never hurt any of us again, but I honestly didn't know if I was capable of doing that.

"We can secure him for now and decide when we get a chance to talk to him," Orpheus interjected, moving forward to pick my father's form off the ground.

"Good idea,' I said, trying to hide the lump in my throat and the indecision in my soul.

"Let's go home," Athena said, reaching for her mate's hands.

I followed behind them, their giddy cheeriness palpable, but I couldn't help but feel the weight of those words.

Home.

I didn't have a home, not anymore. Shockgrove could have been, maybe, if I had enough time. My sister was here, and her family was. I could have been happy here. This place could have become home to me someday, but that thought was thwarted by the climbing vine of ivy on my forearm and the promise I had made.

I wouldn't take it back, even if I could, but a selfish, lonely part of me wondered if I'd ever find a place to call 'home.'

ATHENA

EIGHT

There was only one word to describe how I felt now that the battle with the Hunters was done.

Relief.

I wasn't naive enough to assume we were entirely out of danger. Dr. Kline Galvin's absence from the lighthouse battle was notable. I'm sure he'd be here, with reinforcements of his own, and we would tackle that when it happened, but I also knew the importance of celebrating the little wins. And right now, this was a little win.

I didn't want to think about the promise Davia had to make to secure us the victory, but if Orpheus trusted this Elias guy enough to ask him to help us, then I trusted him to take care of her while she fulfilled her promise to them. Archer looking out for her definitely lifted a weight off my chest.

She was going to be ok. They both were. And because of their promise, we had won the battle even if the war was far from over.

We walked Davia home. I offered for her to stay with me, but she waved me off. "As if I want to hear you getting railed by your sexy vampires? No, thank you, I'm perfectly fine here," she added. I hugged her again, whispering my thanks

She deflected them all, telling me that she would do anything in the world for me. I told her the same.

"Promise me you'll come see me before you go," I demanded into her hair as I embraced her.

"I recently learned to be wary of that word, but I will. I swear." She winked and disappeared into her home. I looked over at Archer, who watched after her with yearning alight in his eyes. I wasn't going to press him on it, but I was glad to know she would be there with someone who seemed to care for her as I did.

Orpheus carried the limp body of my father to The Maine Plotline, careful to avoid the cameras that the police divulged were on the pier. I didn't comment aloud on the irony of tying him up in my office as I had once been tied up in his, but it didn't escape me.

"He'll be out for a while. Ronan packs one hell of a punch," Silas mused, almost admiring the red-headed fae's handiwork.

"I'll guard him tonight," Archer said.

"I'll stay with you," Silas chimed in. The two shared a look of camaraderie, and my heart warmed at the sight.

"Call us if you need anything," Orpheus commanded, indicating the phone on the desk. Silas nodded before coming over to me.

"Get some rest, bookworm. Don't let those rabid animals keep you up with their mouths on your pussy all night," he teased with a sinful look in his eyes.

Archer gagged, smacking Silas' arm. "What did I say about saying those things in front of me? Fucking hell, Silas…" He stalked off toward the front desk, shaking his head as if trying to dispel the mental image, and I watched him leave, chuckling.

"You did that on purpose," I scolded playfully. He acted offended, pressing a hand against his chest.

"Who me? Never." he smiled, sweeping me up into a spinning embrace. His lips met mine as he slowly lowered me to the ground. His tongue dipped into my mouth, and he moaned as our tastes mingled. His hands tangled in my hair, and my breasts pressed against his hard chest.

"I love you so much, Silas," I vowed against his lips. He glanced down at me, his arms caging me against his body, and smiled so warmly that I felt the icy chill of my skin slip away under his gaze.

"Hmm, say it again," he commanded softly.

I pressed a kiss to his lips. "I." Kiss. "Love." Kiss. "You." Kiss. He smiled into my kiss and drank me up.

"Go, we will watch him tonight. This can all wait for tomorrow," he promised, and I traced a finger along the slight stubble on his jawline, trailing down his chest and then his arms. My fingers trailed along the inky swirls of his tattoos and stopped just above the raised white lines of my mate mark. A blooming rose. I traced it, loving how my bond with him seemed to alight within my chest as I did. He leaned down, pressing his lips to his mark on my chest, and we both groaned as the bond pulsed deliciously.

"We're definitely going to be experimenting with that later," he teased, flicking his tongue along my collarbone where his serpents were. The moan that escaped me was entirely involuntary.

"We will see you tomorrow, Silas. One of us will come to relieve you," Orpheus said, patting him on the back and throwing an arm around my shoulders.

"Take good care of our girl," he called out as we stepped away.

"Always," Orpheus replied, pulling me closer to his side.

Laz and Samara trailed behind us as we returned to my cottage. I glanced only briefly over at the lighthouse. Standing sentinel and abandoned as if it hadn't just been the sight of a massive battle with countless casualties.

If I thought about it long enough, I'd find myself feeling queasy and sick at the thought of all those lives lost, but they made their choice. They chose hate. They would rather follow a cause mindlessly than consider that they might be wrong. My father was wrong. About me, about The Wanderers, about the supernatural. His Hunters were fighting for the wrong side, and I wished it could have been different. I wished it didn't have to come to that.

That lighthouse had seen far too much death.

One death that broke my heart and the others that set me free.

When we arrived back at my little house, I eagerly rushed in and disrobed. The scent of blood was thick in the air, and I couldn't bear to be covered in it a moment longer.

"Clothes off," I ordered to my mates.

"Silas told us to behave," Laz jested, but they made quick work of the button of their pants.

"I don't want you three trailing blood over my house," I retorted, turning to face them. All three of them had gone still, their eyes glued to my naked form.

I rolled my eyes, playfully annoyed at their distractability.

"Clothes, now," I repeated before turning on a heel to head for the shower. "I have room for one more in the shower with me for whoever listens the fastest."

I didn't bother turning to see if they had heeded my offer, but I heard the tell-tale rustling of clothes and a few choice curses as elbows were thrown. I chuckled as I turned the shower faucet and let the water heat to an appropriate temperature, which I was learning in my new vampire form wasn't quite as scalding as I used to prefer but was now a more comforting lukewarm.

I slipped inside the shower to stand beneath the running water, averting my eyes from the blood running down my body and circling the drain. I just focused on the feel of the water as it danced on my skin. I heard someone approach and slide in the shower behind me, but I didn't turn to see who it was. I didn't have to. As their hands slid around my waist, I felt my bond with Laz flicker to life within my chest at their nearness.

"You won the race," I mused, leaning my head back onto their chest. Their hands circled my body and held me tight against them.

"Orpheus is fuming," they boasted, and I laughed.

The water poured over our bodies, rinsing us clean from the horrific events of the last few hours. The steam rose around us, wrapping us in a warm, hazy embrace that starkly contrasted the chaos we had just survived. I closed my eyes, letting the water cascade over my face, and tried to let the tension melt away. But my mind was a whirlpool of memories and emotions, each one clamoring for attention. The past few days have been challenging, to say the least.

"You wanna tell me what's on your mind?" Laz whispered into my ear, and I sighed softly.

"It's been a rough few days," I admitted. The confession only scratches the surface of the emotional turmoil swirling inside me.

"You could say that again," they agreed. Their fingers trailed delicate lines along my hips.

"I'm okay, though," I promised.

"You don't have to mince words with me, Athena. It's okay if you're not okay." They rested their chin on my shoulder and hugged me tight to their body. I gripped their arms, which were wrapped around me and held tightly. Their support felt so comfortable that the small wall I'd built around my emotions began to crumble, and tears fell freely from my eyes, mingling with the water pouring over our heads.

"He didn't want me," I wept, admitting the words out loud felt even harsher than when they were nagging at my heart.

Laz's arms tightened around me, spinning me in their arms to face them. I buried my head into their chest and cried, the sobs wracking my body with a force I couldn't control. Laz's hand stroked my hair, their touch gentle and soothing.

"It's okay to cry," they whispered. "But just know that he doesn't deserve your tears."

I clung to them, the warmth of their body grounding me in the moment. "It just hurts so much," I choked out. "He chose his stupid obsession over me. Over both of us." There it was, the heart of it. He hadn't just left me. He left my mother. The kindest soul I'd ever known. He chose hate and violence over a life with us, and it crushed her.

Laz's arms wrapped tighter around me, their embrace a fortress against the pain. "He's a damn fool," they said softly. "It is his loss that he will never know the amazing woman you have become. The woman your mother raised you to be."

Their words broke something open inside me, and the tears came even harder. I let myself cry and mourn the loss of the father I never knew. Laz held me through it all, their presence unwavering.

"I don't know if I can kill him if it comes to that," I admitted, my voice muffled against their chest. "But what if he won't see reason? What if he still wants to hurt us? What do I do then?"

Laz pulled back slightly, tilting my chin up so that I had to meet their gaze. Their eyes were filled with an intensity that took my breath away. "You don't have to make that choice alone, Athena. We're in this together. Every step of the way."

I nodded, trying to believe them. "I feel like I'm drowning."

"Then let us be your lifeline," Laz said firmly. "Lean on us. Lean on me. We won't let you drown."

Their gentle caress gave me a glimmer of hope. I took a shaky breath, trying to steady myself. "I need you," I whispered against their skin.

"You have me," Laz said, their voice fierce with conviction. "Always."

I clung to that promise, letting it anchor me. The water continued to pour over us, but the storm inside me began to calm.

"Thank you," I whispered, my voice still trembling but filled with gratitude.

Laz kissed my forehead, their lips warm and reassuring.

As the water washed away the remnants of the battle, I felt a spark of hope reignite within me.

"Kiss me," I pleaded, and they gave me the slightest nod before pressing their lips to mine. Their kiss has always been more calm, more simmering. I relished in the slow build of passion as their hands slid around my waist and pulled me taut against their torso. I felt their length harden against my stomach, and a small whimper of excitement escaped my lips.

"Laz," I moaned against their lips as the inferno of their slow and steady kiss was getting torturous.

"Yes, darlin'?" They asked teasingly.

"I need you," I repeated, but this time with a much darker and sinful connotation. They smirked.

"I'm yours," they confessed, leaning down to lift me and hitch my legs around their hips. I yelped as the ground disappeared below me, and I was pressed up against the wall of the shower. My limbs wound tightly around their frame. "You know, I love sharing you with Silas," they began, sliding a hand between us toward the apex of my thighs. "I love watching him slam into you and having him tell me exactly what to do to make you scream." Their finger brushed ever-so-slightly over my clit, and I bucked against their hold, but they didn't give me any more than that. Just a delicate touch that was so gentle I almost cried out. "But you and I, like this…" they whispered, sliding their finger through my folds and eliciting a dirty moan from my lips. "These quiet moments where there's nothing else but the two of us, our bodies, our souls." They slid a finger into my heat, and my head fell back to rest against the tiles behind me. They teased me for a few moments, drawing their finger out of me at a deliciously sinful pace before pressing in again. My body was so tightly wound I was nearly about to explode. They withdrew and reached down to grip their length and notched it at the entrance of my pussy.

"This is my happy place," they said as they thrust inside of me. I groaned and cried out their name. My nails dug into their shoulder blades as I circled my hips and pressed down against them.

We made love there against the shower wall, with no sense of rush or reckless abandon, just slow, sensual, and purposeful thrusts. Their body joined to mine in a way so intimate it almost brought a tear to my eye. I let my tongue run along the mark at their throat, my rose, and they shivered at the sensation.

"Please, do that again," they demanded softly. So I did. I let my lips and tongue worship the piece of their skin that now belonged to me, and their breathless moans told me that they loved every second of it. They shifted so that their fingers could dance along my hip where the phases of the moon were forever embedded on my body, and the moment our marks were both being worshiped at the same time, the bond pulsed within us, sending a shock of ecstasy through my body and sent me toppling into a climax. Laz's thrust sped up, and they grunted their release with my name on their lips.

When our breathing returned to normal, I felt it—the single beat of our hearts, synchronized and strong. My smile stretched across my face. They slowly lowered me so that my feet hit the shower floor but kept their hold on me until I was steady enough to stand on my own.

We washed each other off then, taking turns exploring each other's bodies while rinsing away the grime and memories of the day.

When the water began to turn cold, I begrudgingly suggested that we leave so the others could shower as well. Instantly feeling guilty, I asked them to strip out of their clothes and then left them without a shower for over a half hour.

I'm so sorry. We're almost done. I projected to Samara and Orpheus.

Don't be sorry. That's my favorite sound in the world. Orpheus replied smugly.

We are more than content to wait, love. Take the time you need in there. I could tell that she didn't just mean time to shower. She must have recognized the pain I was in and the aggravation I needed to work out.

Laz hopped out of the shower and brought me a towel, wrapping me tightly before doing the same. We exited into the bedroom, and I smiled, seeing Oprheus and Samara standing facing the opposite direction, entirely naked, not sitting so they didn't get my furniture messy.

"Oh my god, I'm so sorry," I chuckled. "The bathroom is all yours."

Samara smiled thankfully. "I'll be quick," she promised, jogging past me into the room. Laz excused themself, averting their eyes from the other two, and disappeared into the living room, leaving me alone with Orpheus. I turned my attention to him. His eyes trailed the water droplets that traveled across my skin, running down the valley of my breasts. His gaze was so heated that I almost felt the water itself burn me under his supervision. I took this moment to appreciate his naked form. I never really took the appropriate amount of time to just stare at my mates. Something I planned to rectify immediately. They were all beautiful. Like stunningly so. His shoulders were broad and toned, while the planes of his stomach were hard and rigid. He, like Laz, bore scars from a time before I knew him. And judging by the age he had only ever really alluded to, it was a time long before. His hair was tousled from the fight, but he looked as if he had rinsed off the blood that had splattered his face and exposed skin off in the sink.

I stepped forward, standing before his bare form, with only a towel between us.

"I have something for you," he professed softly. I smiled up at him.

"I don't need anything," I whispered, the truth in my statement ringing out in the air between us.

"You do, and I want to be the one to give it to you." He reached over to my bedside table where a blue cloth-bound journal sat. My eyebrows furrowed as I looked at it. He held it out in between us.

"A journal?" I asked, gripping the gift in my hands. He nodded gently, a look of guilt crossing his features.

"I told you briefly about the…unfortunate side effects of our nature," he started, and my breath caught in my throat. "I have lived a very long time. And I do not regret this new existence of mine. It brought me to my family. It brought me to you." He reached up to grip my arms, tears cresting in his eyes. "But what I do regret is that I never wrote it down—the life I had before. I have no recollection of my family or who I was before I was this. I don't know if I had any siblings, if I played with them if I got along with them… I don't know if I had a father who taught me how to be a man. I don't know if I had a mother who loved me." The tear slid down his cheek, and I felt the familiar sting in my eyes as I let his words sink in. One day, I would forget my mother, too. "I have no recollection of being turned. Did I ask for it? Was it my choice? It's all gone because I never took the time to remember it while I still could." Regret was painted so clearly on his face.

He reached for the cover of the journal in my hands and drew it open to the first page.

'Remembering Francesca Landry'

The words scrawled in small letters tore me apart at the seams. Tears poured down my face. I pulled the journal close to my chest, already feeling an emotional connection.

"Write it all down, Athena. Tell her story in these pages so she will live forever alongside you," he vowed, and all I could do was nod. This gift was something so sweet and yet so perfectly sentimental.

"I can't express how much this means to me. Thank you," I replied, my voice hoarse and full of emotion.

He leaned forward to bring his lips to mine. I leaned into the gentle and comforting kiss. The journal was pressed against my heart and pinned between the two of us—a perfect place for it.

Samara slipped out of the shower, a towel wrapped around her glistening body, and smiled at me.

"You gave it to her?" she indicated to the journal between us.

Orpheus nodded.

"Good. I look forward to learning more about the woman who made you who you are." My heart constricted with love. There was something so incredibly beautiful about the people I loved, wanting to know about the person who loved me before they could.

"Thank you, " I repeated. Orpheus kissed my forehead before side-stepping me and entering the bathroom.

Samara squeezed my hand before slipping out of the room, leaving me alone with the empty journal.

I discarded the towel and quickly donned an oversized t-shirt before sliding onto my bed and opening the journal to the second page. My pen hovered over the page hesitantly. There was so much I never wanted to forget about my mother, so many moments and joyful memories that I desperately wanted to cling to. Where would I even start?

I guess the best place to start is with the most important.

Athena,

If you're reading this, it means you're starting to forget your mother. The way her smile lit up a room, the way her eyes crinkled when she laughed, the warmth in her embraces, and the love she felt for you—so let me remind you.

These pages will one day be filled with specific memories, moments in time that you shared together that impacted who you became. There will be stories about your inside jokes and the joy of sharing your family business. The strength she had to protect you and to stand up for you even when it meant her own heart was shattered. We will get to all that, the good, the bad, and the ugly, because remembering it all is important. To know that she was always there through every wonderful and painful memory.

But there is one thing that, even if you forget all those stories and all those memories, you should know. Something you should always be aware of no matter how far removed you get from your human life.

Your mom loved you.

She loved you with a love so fierce and so powerful that you felt empowered to take on the world as long as she was by your side. She loved you so completely that you never felt the absence of your father as void. She loved you in a way that made you strong.

The memories are important. The stories matter. But if you only remember one thing, let it be that you were loved.

My tears slid down my cheeks, staining the pages of the journal as I wrote. My mates allowed me these quiet moments alone with my journal and the memory of my mother. A few hours later, my hand was cramped, and a dozen or so pages were filled with some of my favorite memories of growing up with my mom.

The creaking floorboard had my head snapping up to see who was there. Orpheus leaned against the doorframe, wearing a tight white tee and loose-fitting flannel pajama pants. I smiled at the relaxed nature of it.

"How long was I writing for?" I asked, looking over at the clock on the bedside table.

"Couple hours, it's nearly morning," he admitted. I smiled, sliding my new favorite journal into the bedside drawer, then sliding under the covers. I glanced over at him.

"You joining me?" I asked, holding open the comforter. He smirked and sauntered over to slide in beside me. Nestling beneath the comforters, I curled up next to his muscular frame, resting my head on his chest. We lay in silence for a few moments, and I took a moment to count his heartbeats. Silas had once described his heart rate as 'racing' around me. Which, for a vampire, it was. I lay on his chest, breathing as he breathed, letting his infrequent heartbeat comfort me.

"Thank you for giving me a way to remember her," I said, breaking the silence. His fingers traced idle lines along my back as he replied.

"I wish someone had been there to tell me to do the same," he mused.

"Do the others keep journals?" I asked.

He shook his head. "Samara doesn't have an enjoyable history. She never deemed it worth remembering. In fact, I think she often wishes for time to speed up so that she will wake up one day and finally forget what her parents did to her."

Those people were monsters. How could they have done that to my perfect Samara? My heart broke for my mate and her pain.

"You know Laz's story, they would rather forget the pain and betrayal, and I honestly get it. Their scars, though, those act as an unwritten journal. A vicious map of those memories. I'm afraid they'll never truly forget what they did to them. No matter how desperately they may wish to."

My hold tightened on my mate, sending a pulse of love down the bond I shared with Laz. They answered back by tugging on the bond, bringing a smile to my face.

"Silas brought the only person he cared for from his previous life with him, so he didn't need to remember anything else."

I instantly felt guilt and pain surfacing. How was it that I had so much worth remembering and my mates didn't? It wasn't fair.

"Hey, hey, whatever you're thinking…cut it out," he said, reaching for my chin and lifting my eyes to meet his.

"You have your powers turned on?" I asked.

"Not right now, I just know you, little nymph."

I snuggled into his side. His fingers danced along my hip, brushing slightly along the exposed skin where my t-shirt had bunched up.

"You really do," I mused. "I feel like I've known you all for my whole life. Is that a mate thing?" I asked.

"That's a love thing," he confessed.

"Kiss me," I begged, and he obliged, leaning his head to meet my lips with his. It was soft, lazy, and exploratory. We didn't rush but instead took a moment to really feel each other's kiss and commit the feeling to memory. My core tightened, and I felt myself growing wetter the more his mouth devoured mine.

After a long while of just exploring each other, he pulled back. "You should get some rest." I may have pouted because he chuckled softly, shifting me around so that my back was pressed against his front. He pulled me tight against him, his arms circling my waist and holding me in place.

"No fair," I whined.

"You told us you needed three to five business days," he teased. "And Laz already broke the rule."

"It was supposed to be a joke," I grumbled beneath my breath, and his body shook behind me with laughter.

"You're insatiable," he commented coyly.

"Well then, I guess it's a good thing I have four of you to satiate me," I tossed back with feigned aggression. He laughed again, the sound melodic and intoxicating.

"Go to sleep, little nymph," he ordered softly.

"I'm actually thinking I might go find Samara," I taunted, shifting to get up, but his arms closed around me tighter.

"You wouldn't dare," he whispered playfully against my ear.

"Watch me," I teased, wiggling my backside against his growing erection. He released a deep growl.

"You want my cock inside of you? Is that it?" He asked, all playfulness replaced by pure, intense lust.

"Yes, please," I replied with a giggle, like a damn sex-starved woman. His hands danced along the bare skin of my thigh, nearing my apex with each tortuous pass. After a few passes without any relief, I swirmed, pressing my ass into him again. "Touch me," I begged.

"Patience will be rewarded, little nymph," he promised, smirking against my throat.

He continued his vicious exploration of my body, trailing his fingers so near to where I desperately needed him but never quite bridging the gap. It may have been minutes or hours, but by the time he let his fingers brush against the lips of my pussy for the first time, I was a dripping mess, completely lost to my lust.

"You are always so ready for me, aren't you?" he whispered darkly.

I nodded my answer, unable to find my voice amidst the cloud of passion.

"And when I touch you, will I find you soaking wet for me?" He asked, dancing his fingers against the lips but not quite dipping into my heat. I spread my legs, bending my left leg over his hip to give him all the access he needed.

"Yes, I'm so wet for you, Orpheus," I vowed in a whispered cry.

"Guess I'll have to see for myself," he said before sliding his fingers through my wetness to find my clit. I bucked into his touch, every nerve ending so sensitive that I was nearly climaxing already. "Fuck," he whispered in awe. "You are perfect, Athena."

I wanted to reply, I might have, but he stole my words by sliding two fingers directly into my pussy. Stretching me so deliciously that words were a long-forgotten memory to me. He took his time, slowly exploring every inch of me with skillful fingers. I was a wanton blubbering mess by the time he pulled his fingers out and inserted them again, slowly and deliberately.

"More," I begged incoherently.

"Patience," he replied, but his voice was strained, as if he, too, was having a hard time controlling his urges and was reminding not only me but himself. He slid his fingers in and out of me at an achingly deliberate pace. I felt so tightly wound, so impossibly turned on, that the second his thumb pressed against the bundle of nerves at the apex of my thighs, I exploded. My orgasm rippled through my body, and Orpheus held me tightly through it, pumping his fingers in and out to prolong the ecstasy.

"So perfect," he mused as he watched me come undone under his touch.

When I came down from the climax, he didn't remove his fingers but instead continued his relentless pace. I groaned, feeling the tightness in my lower belly return with each punishing stroke of his skilled fingers.

"I love feeling you fall apart in my arms," he confessed sweetly.

"I need you," I begged my voice nothing but a breathless whisper.

He slowly removed his fingers, relishing in each inch. And lined his cock up from behind me. He shifted his hips slightly, giving him perfect access to enter me from his position behind me. But he didn't. He sat there with his tip notched at my entrance and held my hips still so I couldn't squirm down to take him inside of me.

"Orpheus," I cried. "Please."

He pressed his hips forward so achingly slow that each new inch inserted brought with it a shiver of lust and anticipation. When he was finally seated entirely inside of me, my walls stretched around him. He paused, unmoving.

"This is where I belong," he admitted into my hair, his breathing rapid and strained. He circled his hips but didn't move to thrust. I loved how full I felt of him. I felt him in every inch of my body, knowing that was his intention. "I'd look back for you," he whispered, and I turned my head to meet his gaze.

"What?" I said, breathlessly.

"The story of Orpheus and Eurydice," he confirmed. It had been a while since I'd read the story, but I recalled the gist of it. "Hades told them that they could leave the underworld and be together as long as Orpheus never looked back to see if Eurydice was still following him." He circled his hips again, and I moaned at the sensation. "He was so overcome with love, so afraid to lose her, so terrified that she had been left behind, hurt, or lost, that he turned back. He gave up a potential future with her just to ensure her safety in that moment." His lips pressed a kiss against my throat where his mate bond sat. The bond vibrated enticingly, which had me tightening my muscles around him. He moaned. "To love someone is to look back. And I'd look back for you, little nymph," he vowed just before he withdrew his cock and slammed it back into my dripping cunt.

I cried out his name as he finally gave me everything I needed. His cock hit each delicious part of me, which because of his torturous build-up, had been rearing and ready for him. My muscles tightened as I felt the climax build at his now aggressive pace. He held my hips in pace and pressed into me, over and over and over, each thrust filled with more love and promise than the last. He dipped a finger down the front of my stomach and pressed against my clit as he continued to slam into me from his spooning position.

My vision blurred as the climax swept me away. I felt warmth spread down my legs as my release coated his cock. I didn't even have a moment to feel embarrassed because he pulsed into me with reckless abandon, his breathing becoming shallower as he neared his own release.

His hips jerked as he fell apart, and I rode him through it all. A few moments passed before he slowly withdrew from me and helped me up from the now-soiled sheets.

"I'm going to need to buy more sheets if we're going to keep ruining them,"

I whispered. I glanced over at Orpheus, and we devolved into laughter.

"There are several sets on their way already, along with your new bed and a waterproof mattress topper," Samara said, slipping in through the bedroom door with a fresh set of sheets in her hands and I shook my head, trying to piece together what she had just said. Laz was close on their heels, their heated gaze washing over my body before helping Samara strip the mattress.

"I'm sorry, what?" I asked.

"You didn't think the five of us were going to fit on your queen mattress comfortably forever, did you?" Orpheus replied nonchalantly, reaching forward to tuck one corner of the new sheet under the mattress.

"I.. well, I.." I stuttered.

"An Alaskan King should be arriving tomorrow afternoon," Laz excitedly said. "Don't worry. I measured it, and it'll fit."

My gaze bounced back and forth between the three of them. "You bought us a new bed?" I asked.

"Yes," Orpheus replied, smiling. Seemingly amused by my shock.

"And more than enough sheet sets for us to ruin at least two a day," he answered, smirking sinfully.

My eyes stung with tears of pride and joy as I watched three of my mates make my bed. It was such a mundane yet beautiful action.

"You bought us a bed," I repeated, a love-filled sob lodged in my throat. They glanced over at me, mirroring my emotions in their expressions.

"This is forever, Athena," Samara promised, stepping forward to grab my hands in hers. Her soft skin against mine sent a buzz of happiness rushing through me. "We are all in, and this place… this place is your home as long as you want it to be. So, yes, my love, we bought us a bed. One big enough to hold every ounce of our love for you."

I knew we couldn't stay forever, but I hoped it'd be longer than a few days.

I threw my arms around her neck, dragging her into my embrace. Her skin felt silky and smoothed against mine, and I cherished how her perfect curves fit delicately against mine.

I pulled back, meeting her warm brown eyes.

"Thank you," I spoke to her softly. "All of you, thank you so much."

When are you going to realize that we would do absolutely anything for you? Samara whispered into my mind. The corners of my lips lifted into a smile.

I guess I'm just trying to believe that I deserve it. I admitted. She tilted her head, her eyes softening.

You deserve all of it and more. She let her hands dance over my arms, and I felt the warmth of her healing powers seep into my body, mending the bruises that still dotted my skin.

Thank you for kissing it better. I said again, the words I knew I'd be speaking to her for the rest of our eternity.

"We should get some rest," she answered aloud. "Sleep with me tonight?" Samara asked hopefully. I beamed back at her.

"You heard the lady," I said, raising my voice for the others to hear but keeping my eyes from hers. "She's got dibs tonight."

Laz and Orpheus feigned disappointment, but I saw the look on their faces when they saw how Samara was looking at me. The way she held me. The way she loved me. They were once afraid she'd never feel that way again. They were happy for her.

Once the others vacated the room to make their beds on the various couches in my living room, I gripped my mate's hand and led her to the freshly made bed.

We settled in, comfortably entangled beneath the sheets, our limbs and bodies eager to keep the other as close as possible.

"What are you thinking about?" I asked, studying the contemplative look on her face. She smiled down at me.

"I'm thinking about how Alora," she replied in a melancholic whisper.

I sighed, tightening my hold on her. "I think about her a lot," I admitted, tracing my finger along her chest where she now bore my mark. The small white lines of the rose stood out so stunningly against the canvas of her unblemished ebony skin. Our bond hummed in my chest.

"You do?" Samara breathed shock in her tone.

I nodded. "All the time." I felt my chest tighten. "I constantly find myself wondering if she was my mate, too. Did I lose her before I ever got to have her? I have no way of knowing, but it hurts to think we may have had what you and I share. That I may have had another person to love if my father gave her the chance."

Samara pulled me closer to her chest.

"I think about that, too," she admitted quietly, stroking my back.

"Tell me about her?" I prompted. I felt her chest rise and fall with a long, painful breath. Her heart beat once beneath my cheek.

"What do you want to know?" She asked, pressing her lips against my hair. Her almost floral scent filled my nostrils, and I inhaled deeply.

"Everything."

And so she did. I listened intently as Samara shared with me the memories of her chosen. Her wife. I laughed with her. I cried with her. I held her hand when it shook and wiped her tears when they blurred her vision.

My heart ached alongside hers for the woman whom my mate loved.

We held each other as she recounted their stories and told me how brave and strong she was. I knew the sun had risen for the day, not by any filtering light. The tint and curtains concealed those, but I could hear the birds sing their song, once a sound that had welcomed me to a new day was now beckoning me to sleep.

"I would have loved her," I whispered, exhaustion overtaking me.

"She would have loved you right back," Samara replied softly as I drifted back to sleep.

ARCHER

NINE

The sun was starting to rise, casting a soft glow through the edges of the heavy curtains in the office of The Maine Plotline. I stood there, staring at my father tied to a chair, waiting for him to regain consciousness. The sight of him bound and helpless brought a storm of mixed feelings, each one crashing against the other.

I leaned tensely against the desk, my fingers drumming absently on its surface. The familiar smell of books and aged wood was comforting, yet the tension in the room was palpable. The quiet was interrupted only by the ticking of the old clock on the wall and the soft rustle of pages as a breeze slipped through a crack in the window. Athena and I created our bond in this store. It was where we became friends. Where we got to know each other, and now it was the place that held the father who betrayed both of us. I hoped his presence wouldn't forever taint my memory of this place. This is where the love for my sister blossomed, and I didn't want him to take that away from me, too.

Looking at my father, I couldn't help but feel a pang of regret. This was the man who had raised me and taught me how to survive in a world that aimed to hurt us. But he was also the man who had been so lost in his crusade that he'd rather hurt those he 'loved' than admit his mistakes.

The ropes around his wrists and ankles looked tight, cutting into his skin, which was pink and raw from them. I wondered if they hurt. I wondered if he cared. He had always been so strong, so unyielding. Seeing him like this felt wrong like I was looking at a ghost of the man I once knew.

I took a deep breath, trying to steady my thoughts. When he woke up, what would I say to him? How could I face him, knowing what he had done? The anger I felt was real, but so was the sorrow. I wanted answers, but I wasn't sure I could handle it if he didn't submit. If he didn't listen.

The clock ticked on, each second stretching into an eternity. I rubbed my temples, feeling the weight of the night's events bearing down on me. This wasn't just about me anymore. It was about Athena, about her newfound family, and all the supernatural lives that had been torn apart by his choices.

His eyelids fluttered, and I straightened, my heart pounding in my chest. This was it. The moment I had dreaded and anticipated in equal measure. He groaned softly, his head lolling to the side before he slowly opened his eyes.

Our gazes locked, and for a moment, neither of us said anything. The silence was deafening. The man before me was a stranger, yet he was my father.

"Dad," I said, my voice barely more than a whisper.

He blinked, recognition dawning in his eyes, followed by a flicker of something I couldn't quite read. Regret? Resignation? Or just the cold, calculating look of a man who had lost control?

"Archer," he replied, his voice hoarse. "What have you done?"

The question hung in the air, heavy and loaded with meaning. What had I done? What had he done? The lines were so blurred I didn't know where to begin.

"We had to stop you," I said finally, my voice stronger.

He didn't respond immediately. He just studied me with those piercing eyes that had once commanded my respect and fear.

"Where is Dr. Galvin?" I asked. I had a million questions to ask him, but the most pressing threat was, without a doubt, the impending arrival of Nameless's elusive and mysterious leader.

My father scowled, his bruised face twisting wickedly. "You know better than to say his name aloud. If he's coming for you, then you won't stand a chance. You'll never see him coming," he spat. "You've chosen the wrong side, kid."

"Don't fucking call me a kid," I warned. His eyes widened in shock.

"I was always hoping you'd finally grow up. Just never thought you'd be so foolish when you did," he said quietly.

"Tell me about the weapon in your drawer. The blade that emulates a vampire bite." If he was surprised I knew about it he didn't show it. "And don't try to deny it. I've seen it."

"What do you want to know?" He said, meeting my gaze.

"Did you kill all those people, the ones in the files? Did you frame The Wanderers?" Tears stung my eyes.

"Fuck no, I'm not a monster, they are!" He retorted.

"Then why do you have that weapon?" I shouted back.

"When Galvin tells you to keep something safe, you do it," he spat. I ran my hands through my hair anxiously.

"You never asked what it was? Why he had it? What it did?" I probed.

His lips were pressed into a hard line. "It wasn't my place," he answered.

"You're kidding me," I spat. "You had proof that he was framing vampires in your damn drawer, and you think it wasn't your 'place' to ask why!?"

"You don't understand.."

"Who is Glavin? Who is he?" I interjected.

"What the fuck are you on about? He's the leader of Nameless, and you know that as well as I do."

"No, Dad, I mean, who the fuck is he? There's nothing about him anywhere. Past fifteen years ago, he was nothing but a ghost. Have you ever even seen him without his mask? Do you even know anything about him?" I was screaming, but I couldn't stop myself if I wanted to.

He started to respond but quickly snapped his mouth shut. His turmoil was reflected in his eyes.

"Silas, I need your help," I called out, knowing the tatted Wanderer was listening. The door to the office creaked open, and the long-haired vamp slipped inside. My father winced, pushing back against his chair in an attempt to put as much space between him and Silas as possible.

"Get him out of here," my father hissed.

"He's not going to hurt you," I promised, tossing an apologetic look at Silas, who was undoubtedly itching to do just that.

"You've aligned yourself with monsters, Archer."

"This *monster*, as you call him, climbed back into the window of Nameless, risking being caught, imprisoned, and tortured for the third time just to carry my beaten and bloodied body out of there after *you* had me nearly beat to death. Tell me, would you rather I be dead?"

Something that resembled guilt flashed in his eyes.

"I'm going to try and prove to you that you're the one who's been fighting for the wrong side," I said, lifting the sleeve of my shirt to expose my wrist. The scar I bore from Evangeline stared up at me.

"Why bother?" He asked.

"Because if you can see reason if you finally see the truth, then maybe I won't have to decide if you need to die."

His breath caught in his throat, and his mouth fell open. He shook his head, tears brimming in his eyes.

"Please, just try to have an open mind," I whispered before holding my arm out for Silas. I hadn't told him my plan, so I hoped he wouldn't be upset with me, but I couldn't think of another way to show my father the proof. I know Athena had mentioned that it was a rather intimate experience, but I had come to trust

Silas. This little display had worked on me, after all. But I wasn't quite as far gone as he seemed to be.

Silas gripped my wrist in his hands, offering me a tight nod before letting his fangs descend and his features shift. My father squirmed in his chair, kicking his feet out to push himself back, but he was stuck. He couldn't move. He had to watch this.

The moment Silas' fangs pierced my skin, I winced, but it wasn't as painful as I remembered it. Maybe my fear had something to do with it. My skin didn't tear or rip as it had when I was wrestling it away from Evangaline's desperate bite. In fact, after the initial sting, if I sat completely still and allowed Silas to drink… it didn't feel painful at all. It felt almost good. Like that tingle, you get when someone plays with your hair. I watched him drink a few thick mouthfuls of my blood before he retracted his fangs and swept his tongue along the wound once before dropping my wrist from his hands.

I held my blood-covered wrist out for my father to see. His eyes were latched onto the two deep puncture wounds and surrounding smaller teeth marks to either side. Together, we watched as the wound closed, shrinking so slowly that it seemed as if nothing were happening at all. Within a few moments, the fresh wound was completely gone, leaving only a tiny blood stain and the scar that had once felt so volatile but now represented something much bigger.

My father looked up at me, glancing between the two of us.

"Impossible," he whispered.

"And yet…" I urged.

"We drink human blood," Silas interjected, his features still more vampire than human. "But we don't take life carelessly. We don't kill aimlessly and without cause. Not all of us, at least. Everybody is capable of evil. You are a case in point. But would you have me eradicate all humans because of the actions of one evil man?" As Silas spoke, his eyes returned to their everyday honeyed shade, and his features softened to reveal the humanity beneath the creature. But

I was starting to recognize that humanity existed in both versions of him. It just looked a little different.

"This isn't right.." My father replied, nearly to himself.

"I know that it's hard to look at a belief you've held for your entire life with a critical lens because that means admitting that you've been wrong. But please, for my sake… For Athena's sake. Can you consider even just for a moment that you may be wrong?" I begged, tears slipping from my eyes, repeating the words that Athena had once said to me.

"She's amazing, dad. She's strong, she's powerful. She has the kind of heart you and I could only ever dream of having." Tears spilled from his eyes. "She turned out amazingly, considering all the shit she had to go through after you left them. After you chose hate over a life with her."

He shook his head, not in defiance, but to stave off the onslaught of emotions.

"One of your Hunters killed her," I whispered, and his eyes snapped up to meet mine, his chest rising and falling quickly.

"She's.. She's dead?" I watched the panic in his eyes, hoping that this moment of fear would be enough to convince him to listen to reason.

"She was," Silas answered through his teeth. Anger poured off of him in waves. I knew he was thankful that she had turned, but he hated the circumstances surrounding it. It wanted it to happen on her own timeline.

"Was? No... You don't mean," he stuttered, his eyes frantically bouncing back and forth between the two of us.

"They saved her," I confessed. My father's face twisted in pain and disgust.

"You turned her?! How could you! You condemned her to a life of misery," he spat, thrashing against his bindings.

"Only if you don't stop this fucking crusade!" I answered crudely. "The only threat to her life now is you, Dad! You!" I shouted, my voice trembling with a mixture of anger and desperation.

He paused at that, his eyebrows pinching together as tears continued to flow from his pained eyes. His shoulders slumped, and for the first time, he seemed smaller, less imposing. The lines on his face deepened as he let my words sink in. For the first time in my life, I felt like maybe he had actually heard what I said.

His lips parted, and he took a shuddering breath. "Archer, I... I never wanted it to come to this," he said, his voice barely a whisper. The raw vulnerability in his tone was something I had never heard before, and it caught me off guard.

I shook my head, trying to process his words.

He took a deep breath, the weight of guilt pressing down on him. Finally, he looked up at me, his eyes full of regret and sorrow.

"I don't know how to look past this," he admitted, his voice barely more than a whisper. "But I don't want to lose you. Either of you."

There was a long pause, the silence filled with our unspoken pain. And then, he said something I had waited my whole life to hear.

"I'm sorry, son."

"That's not enough," I confessed, feeling my chest tighten. "But it's a start."

ATHENA

TEN

I stirred awake to the gentle sensation of lips brushing against my neck, a warm and familiar touch that immediately brought a smile to my face. I didn't open my eyes just yet, savoring the moment. Samara's kisses were soft and lingering, each one sending a delightful shiver down my spine.

"Good morning," I murmured, my voice still husky with sleep.

Samara's lips curved into a smile against my skin. "Morning," she whispered back, her breath warm and sweet.

I finally opened my eyes, slightly turning to meet her gaze. Her deep, enchanting eyes were filled with affection, and I felt my heart swell with happiness. There was a softness in her expression that made me feel cherished and adored.

"You're up early," I said, running my fingers through her dark, silky hair. "Or late, I guess," I amended, glancing at the clock that read eight p.m. I was going to need to get used to this whole nocturnal thing because we weren't going to make it to New Orleans anytime soon with all the shit still going on here.

She shrugged, her kisses trailing up to my jawline. "Couldn't resist waking you up this way."

I chuckled softly, the sound vibrating against her lips. "It's pretty good as wake-up calls go."

Samara leaned back slightly, her hand resting on my chest, fingers tracing lazy patterns on my skin. "How are you feeling?"

I took a moment to assess myself. The past few days' events had been intense, to say the least, but right now, lying here with Samara after last night with my mates, I felt a rare sense of tranquility. "Better now," I replied honestly, reaching up to cup her cheek.

She leaned into my touch, her eyes closing briefly. "Good," she said, opening her eyes again to look at me. "You deserve to feel good."

I smiled, pulling her closer for a kiss. Her lips were warm and inviting, and I lost myself in her sweet, familiar taste. When we finally broke apart, I rested my forehead against hers, feeling an overwhelming sense of gratitude for this moment.

"You deserve to feel good too, you know," I offered coyly, smiling innocently at her.

"Is that so?" She replied playfully.

"Hmm, mmm," I said, sliding beneath the blankets and settling between her legs. Her thighs fell open, revealing her center to me, and I moaned in appreciation when I saw that she was bare and ready for me.

I decorated her thighs with simple little kisses, gentle and prolonged. She sighed breathlessly with each one. My mouth neared her core, and I felt her arch her back.

My tongue darted out to wet my bottom lip, eager to feast on my mate. God, she was perfect. The first swipe of my tongue through her slick arousal had us both groaning. She tasted sweet, a perfect blend of flavor, and I drank her eagerly. Alternating between dipping my tongue into her pussy and sucking her clit. Her hands tangled in my hair as she held me tight to her core. As if I'd ever want to leave. I felt so powerful at that moment to have my mate writhing beneath me, her body shaking as I pleasured her. I was so wet I couldn't stop myself from reaching down and pressing my free hand against my aching clit. The action had me groaning, which only sent more sinful vibrations through her.

My fingers slid into her wetness as my tongue circled her clit, and she cried out, her orgasm tearing through her. I drank every last drop of her eagerly.

She tore the comforter from above me, bathing me in the soft, warm light from the bedside lamp. The look in her eyes could only be described as feral. She gripped my shoulders and directed me to lie on my back with a gentle but forceful push. I gasped at the movement. My head hung just barely off the foot of the bed. My legs spread for her as she pulled the hem of my shirt up. I lifted my shoulders from the bed, expecting her to tear the shirt completely off, but instead, she stopped just above my eyes, sending my sight tumbling into darkness and pinning my arms to the side of my head as she tightened the shirt.

My mouth fell open on a moan.

"You trust me, right?" She asked, kissing my clavicle once she was satisfied with her makeshift blindfold.

"Always," I vowed breathlessly, writhing as Samara's mouth hovered over my heated icy skin. All of my other senses were heightened even beyond their new capabilities. I could hear the shifts in her breath, the way her skin moved against the bedspread, the way her fingers dug into the sheets beside me. My nipples pebbled as her breath dusted over them. Her tongue darted out and took one peak into her mouth, and I arched into it. She suckled softly, applying just enough teeth to drive me wild. My hands balled into fists, desperate to reach for her.

She repeated the attention on the other side, careful not to let any other part of her body touch mine.

"You get your new bed today. I figured we could say goodbye to this one together," she whispered against my stomach as her breath trailed lower and lower.

"Yes. God, yes, please," I rambled.

I heard her shift on the bed, pulling her mouth away from where I needed her, and I groaned. She shifted something around in my bedside drawer, and I felt my body shiver in anticipation. It was such a terrifyingly beautiful thing to be completely at the mercy of my mate. To give myself so completely to her and not feel an ounce of reservation. To have one of my senses dulled, the way it had been *that* night, and still feel like I have all the power.

My mates had given me my life back. They'd erased his vicious touch from my memory and replaced his imprint on my soul with theirs.

I felt a tear of love and gratitude slip from the corner of an eye, and just when I prepared to say something to thank her for what she was doing for me, her tongue slipped between the lips of my pussy, and I bucked against her.

"Fuck," I whispered.

"I intend to," she replied wickedly against my core. Then something phallic shaped and warm pressed against my opening.

"What are.." I asked, wondering briefly if one of my other mates had joined us. But then Samara pressed a button, and the vibrator roared to life against my clit, and I cried out at the feel of it.

"Oh my God," I cried out. Samara pressed kisses against my inner thighs as she held the toy against me. She pushed it there, circling it slightly until my whole body shook. Just when I thought I was going to disappear into oblivion, she pressed the head of the vibrator into me. The moan that slipped through my lips was downright pornographic.

She fucked me with the vibrator, alternating between slow and sensual thrusts and hard and punishing ones. The vibrations echoed through my bones, and I couldn't control my violent shaking as my orgasm built and built within me. Her mouth came down onto my clit, somewhere between worship and punishment, and that was all it took to send me toppling into the climax to end all climaxes.

"Holy shit, Samara," I exclaimed loudly as my release soaked the toy and my mate's face. She kept the toy pressed inside of me but turned off the vicious vibrations to give my body a moment of reprieve.

"Athena," she whispered, her voice soft and admiring. "I wish you could see how perfect you are when you scream my name."

I squirmed under her hold, unable to form coherent thoughts in my post-climax blissed-out state. She gently slid the toy from me, making sure I felt every inch of the removal before I was once again writhing.

I felt the bed shift as she positioned herself over me, her legs entangling with mine. I felt the heat from her exposed core hovering above mine, but she didn't press down to meet me. With a hand, she reached up, slowly removing the blindfold from my eyes and gifting me with the sight of my stunning, naked mate looking down at me from her position of power over me. When my vision was cleared, she still didn't move to close the distance between our bodies. Instead, she just held herself there, tantalizingly close but still too far. Her mocha eyes held mine, and too much passion to explain adequately flowed through us. This was love. Passion. Lust. Healing. Safety. She was all of this for me, and by the depths of the look she was giving me, I knew that I was all this for her, too.

"Make love to me, Samara," I whispered. She brought her lips down onto mine and locked my mouth into a passionate exploration before slowly lowering her core to press against mine. We moaned into each other's mouths at the first brush of friction. She maneuvered her hips expertly, chasing her passion and bringing me to the brink of mine. Our breath mingled, coming out in pants. Her breasts pressed against mine, and I let my hands explore them, delicately playing with each peak as her pussy slid against mine.

"Oh fuck," I cried out as my stomach tightened and the orgasm crested.

"That's it, baby. Come for me," she begged, thrusting her hips faster. I threw my head back, arching against the foot of the bed, my hands clasping around her neck and holding her into place as I circled my hips to grind against hers.

"Oh my god," I think I said, but it may have been incoherent as the cascade of euphoria claimed me, toppling me into a body-shaking orgasm. Samara rode me through my climax, her body tense as she chased her own release. She met me at the cliff, and together, we dove off into the ravine of pleasure below. I'm not sure we could have held each other tighter if we tried. When our breathing returned to normal and the delicious tension in our bodies melted away, Samara slid onto the bed beside me, smiling up at me with an exhausted, sated smile.

"Good morning," I whispered, chuckling. She laughed, burying her head in the crook of my neck.

"Good morning," she replied softly.

We lay there for what felt like hours, and simultaneously not long enough.

"I need to see my father," I admitted quietly to the room's darkness. Samara's gentle touch slid against my arm in comfort.

"I know," she said.

We slid off the bed, and I already missed the warm haven of safety while I prepared myself both emotionally and physically for the long evening ahead of me.

I slid into one of my comfortable sweat sets, soft heather grey pants that hugged my curves while still remaining loose and comforting, and a matching cropped hooded sweatshirt. I sat down and allowed myself the simple joy of applying a full face of makeup for the first time since before I was captured. I hadn't realized how much I missed the creative outlet makeup had become for me until I no longer had it. As I painted my eyelids and contoured my cheeks, I thought about how this makeup felt almost like a shield– something to help me brave my next task.

I tamed the wild red strands of my hair into a low ponytail, and finally, I was ready to face my father.

Stepping into the living room, I found Laz and Samara sitting at the island. They each had a mug in front of them, and I could scent the blood all the way from where I stood. Samara slid another mug over to me. I gripped the cup in my hands and marveled at how normal this felt despite the contents as I drank down the delicious liquid. I wasn't used to drinking human blood yet, but the coppery taste still shocked me when it hit my lips. While vampire blood from my mates had all the flavor of human blood, maybe even more so, it did little to quench the hunger in the pit of my stomach. Like eating all the mouthwatering and decadent sweets in the world, it clearly had a superior taste but was not sustainable. Blood from the bag was, of course, not the same as from the vein - thanks to Davia, I knew that now - but it was enough to keep the stabbing hunger that always lay beneath the surface at bay.

"Where's Orpheus?" I asked. Samara and Laz shared a tense look. "What's going on?" Panic rose in my chest as I reached down the bond of him. The fear settled slightly as I felt him there on the other end.

"He's searching for Greg," Laz replied. My breath caught.

"What?" I stuttered.

"He's a potential threat, and in case you haven't noticed, Orpheus is a little bit obsessed about protecting you," Samara added.

"Has he found anything?" I asked.

"Not sure, we haven't had a chance to get new phones yet," Laz shrugged. I instantly sent out a thought to my mate.

Are you ok? Why are you doing that alone? Have you found anything? My nervous stream of consciousness spilled through my mind.

Good morning, Athena. Orpheus replied teasingly. *Yes, I'm perfectly well. I'm just gathering some intel and following trails, and I'm perfectly capable of doing that alone. And not yet, but I won't give up.*

I sighed, feeling the tension in my shoulders relax.

Please be careful. I pleaded.

You don't need to worry about me, little nymph.

I will anyway. I promised.

I know. He replied, and I felt him tugging on the bond, sending a wave of love and warmth down the bond to my heart.

I nodded, releasing a long breath, and leaned against the island before me.

"Are you ready?" Laz asked, coming behind me and caging me against the island with their strong arms.

"As ready as I can be."

They slid my ponytail to one side and pressed a kiss against the back of my neck. I turned to face them and pressed a soft kiss on their willing lips.

"Alright, let's do this," I said, gathering as much bravado as possible.

Together, we strolled through the evening streets of Shockgrove, my footsteps echoing off the familiar buildings. It was early summer, and already tourists were trickling into town, their presence a reminder that these peaceful streets would soon be filled with noise and activity. The thought made my chest tighten. I needed the tension with the Hunters to be resolved soon. The idea of innocent people being caught in the crossfire of my war was too much to bear.

My heart pounded in my chest as I approached the pier and my bookstore. I was nervous beyond anything I'd ever experienced. It's not every day that you need to confront the father that kidnapped you. Facing him was inevitable, and I couldn't keep putting it off. I took a deep breath, trying to steady my nerves, and reminded myself that I wasn't the vulnerable little baby that he left behind. I was stronger now, and I had my mates and my brother. I had a whole life filled with love and earned strength that he didn't get to be a part of.

As I walked, I noticed the early signs of summer everywhere—the vibrant green leaves on the trees, the colorful flowers blooming in the gardens, the warm, bright stars dotting the infinite landscape of the sky, and the gentle breeze that carried the scent of the ocean. Normally, these sights and smells would comfort me, but today, they only reminded me of a home that was tarnished by my father's hate.

A few people passed us on the pier as they closed up shop and headed in for the night, and I envied them for a brief moment. They had already lived their day in the sun and light and were retreating to darkness to sleep, and yet my day was only just beginning.

As I reached the front door to The Maine Plotline, I hesitated for just a moment before pushing open the door. I was shocked to see the 'Open' sign flipped and a few figures inside with arms full of books. My shock doubled when I saw Silas behind the cafe counter, my baby blue half-apron tied around his waist. He got the last croissant from the display case and handed it to the middle-aged woman while Archer ran the cash register. The two worked in perfect synchronicity, smiling and laughing with the customers while sending them on their way. They hadn't noticed us yet, and the smile that was plastered on my face was impossibly large.

I held the door for the two customers as they exited with their goodies, smiles on their faces.

"Thank you, dear," the woman said, smiling at me, which made the soft wrinkles at the corner of her eyes even more prominent. She was gorgeous—a beautiful example of aging gracefully. The gentleman, her husband, I presumed, nodded his thanks to me and then slung his arms over her shoulder, and the two of them walked down the pier, stumbling playfully as they laughed and joked with each other. My heart warmed. I was lucky, I got to spend a different kind of forever with my mates, but there was a certain beauty to growing old with the people you love that felt so enchanting. I'd never see the way grey hair would look on Orpheus, the way Samara's skin would soften, the wrinkles that might decorate Laz's face, or how Silas' tattoos would fade beautifully into his skin.

I wouldn't trade my version of eternity for anything, but I appreciated the reminder that every eternity is different, and none is more beautiful than the other.

The welcome bell echoed through the shop as we slipped inside. I smiled at the two behind the counter, my heart full of warmth.

"You opened the shop today?" I stated, my voice cracking with emotion. Silas came around the counter, sliding off the apron and wrapping me in a hug.

"Of course we did," he whispered against my hair.

"We know this place is important to you, and well, you showed me how to work most of it when I spent time here with you, so it was a no-brainer." Archer reminded me. The images of the lazy afternoons spent in this very shop getting to know the man I had no idea was my little brother returned to me. Less tainted as they had once been. Maybe one day I'd look at those memories fondly without the dark cloud of the Hunters marring it.

"Thank you both," I said, sliding out of Silas' hug to embrace Archer. He held me tightly, sighing with relief, like he felt that I might finally decide I'd had enough at any second and choose to hold his mistakes against him.

"Bold of you to open for business with a hostage in the back office," Laz jested as they flipped the sign to 'Closed' and locked the door, but I could see the actual nerves beneath the humor-filled words.

"We had a little chat with him this morning. He knew to keep quiet if he wanted a chance to speak to you," Archer started nodding to me. I glanced between the two of them.

"And?" I prompted.

"And," Silas began. "Your little ex-hunter here thought it'd be a fun little trick to make me drink from him right in front of dear old dad."

A shocked gasp escaped my lips.

"Well, that's one way to rip the band-aid off," Samara acknowledged under her breath.

"What did he do?" I asked.

"He's got a lifetime of ingrained beliefs to sort through. It's not a switch that can just be flipped. I didn't even buy into the whole 'vampires are evil' idea all that much, and it still took me some time to sort it all out," Archer stated. I nodded. "But he was certainly shaken."

Shaken was good. Shaken meant that the foundation he built his lies on was unsteady and could be rebuilt with the right truths.

I didn't want him as a father. I didn't need him. I already had a mother who meant the world to me, and I was not looking to replace her. But I didn't want to kill him. I wanted his beliefs to change for Archer's sake. I wanted to spare my brother the pain of needing to decide his fate or losing him.

"We can work with that," I expressed before taking a few steps toward the closed office door.

"Want backup, bookworm?" Silas asked as I brushed past him.

I shook my head. "No, thank you. I need to face this alone," I admitted before letting my hand settle on the doorknob.

The door creaked open, and I was met with my father's familiar yet weary, face. His eyes widened in surprise at the sight of me, and for a brief moment, we just stared at each other. Then, taking another deep breath, I stepped inside and closed the door behind me.

My father sat tied up in the chair, his face a twisted mask of anger and desperation. He looked up as I entered, his eyes scanning me with a mixture of confusion, disappointment, and something else I couldn't quite place.

"What a difference just a few days will make," he mused. "It appears we have switched places."

"The only difference is that you deserve to be tied to that chair," I chided back but took a slow breath, trying to compose myself. I needed to remain calm for this if I was going to accomplish what I'd come here for. To change his mind about us.

"You're one of them now," he whispered, and my fists clenched at my side. He said it in a tone so accusatory that I could almost taste the judgment.

"Because your Hunters killed me," I retorted calmly. I couldn't look at him, so I quickly turned and glanced at the books that lay on the desk beside me, letting their worn covers ground me.

"It was never my intention for that to happen," he whispered, and the genuine regret in his tone had caught me off guard. "I only ever wanted what was best for you, Athena. Even before you were born."

I shook my head. "You believed leaving us behind to commit murder was what was best for me?" I bit cooly.

"I believed that leaving you both to protect you from monsters who could harm you was," he replied.

I sighed. Disappointment for the man before me coursed through my veins. "Well, you were right about one thing," I started. "I was better off without you, your hateful rhetoric, and frankly cowardice views. Leaving me to be raised alone by my mother was the greatest thing you could have done for me. So perhaps, for that, I should thank you."

"Does she know that you're one of them? One of those inhumane creatures?" He asked, and I felt a jolt of pain in my heart. Grandma had told me that he didn't know about her death, and for the briefest moment, I felt a sting of pity for my father.

I crossed my arms, leaning against the doorframe, trying to steady my breath and mask the storm of emotions swirling inside me. "I can't believe you can't see the humanity in me," I replied, my voice colder and sharper than I intended, like a shard of ice.

He struggled against his bonds, his frustration etched deeply into the lines of his face. "How can I when you're part of the very thing I've spent my life fighting against?"

I shook my head, stepping closer, feeling the cold seeping from the wooden floorboards into my veins. "I can't see any humanity in you either."

His eyes narrowed, his anger flaring like wildfire. "Does she know?"

I shook my head, trying to fight the sting of tears.

"Because you're ashamed to tell her because you know it's wrong!" He spat.

"No," I whispered, but he continued.

"She may have a soft spot for the creatures, but she wouldn't want her own daughter subjected to a half-life!"

At that, something inside me snapped like a brittle twig. "She's dead!" I blurted out, the words ripping from my throat before I could stop them.

The room fell into a heavy, suffocating silence. My father froze, his eyes widening in shock, the anger in his expression melting into a look of raw, unfiltered pain. "What...?" he whispered, the fire in his voice replaced by a tremor of disbelief.

"She's dead," I repeated, my voice softer now but no less pained, each word like a dagger twisting in my heart. "Cancer. Few years ago now."

The news hit him like a sledgehammer, and I could see the impact of my words in the way his face crumpled, the lines of his features sagging under the weight of the revelation. He cared about her. That much was clear. But he had cared about his crusade against vampires more. And for that, I wasn't sure I could ever forgive him.

He looked up at me, his eyes filled with a sorrow that mirrored my own, a silent reflection of the pain and loss we both carried. "I'm sorry," he said, the words I had unknowingly waited my whole life to hear. "I'm so sorry, Athena."

We just sat there for a moment, the weight of our shared grief hanging heavy in the air like a thick fog.

"I know I couldn't be the father you needed, not when your mother and I disagreed on something so fundamental," he continued, his voice cracking. "You deserved so much better than me. I admit I was glad when your grandma told me that Franny had moved on— that you finally had someone to fill the role I couldn't— I was a little jealous." My chest tightened in response to the prickling fear at the mention of him.

Suddenly, the floodgates opened. I felt the tears I had held back for so long spill down my cheeks. My defenses crumbled, and I let out a shuddering sob. My mates had done such a great job of keeping the vicious memories of him at bay, but here they were, slipping back into my mind like an unwelcome visitor.

Whiskey. White teeth. Selfish hands. My step-father and what he took that did not belong to him. The snapshots of the worst night of my life flashed in rapid succession. His haunting face reminded me of just how helpless I felt, and despite the new power flowing in my veins, I felt like that powerless little girl all over again.

The memories felt so violently real and vibrant after all this time. I don't know why, but my vision flashed with a golden light, and I couldn't stop it. I felt the memory almost project from within me, finding purchase in my father's mind. It was like a rush of emotions, and the images poured out. The dark room, the harsh words, the physical and emotional torment I had endured. I was sharing my pain, my trauma. He saw it and felt everything, just as I had.

The vulnerability of sharing those memories hit me hard. It was as if I was exposed, and every painful moment laid bare not just for my father but for the world. My breath hitched, and for a brief moment, I felt like I was spiraling, losing myself in the trauma all over again.

But then, like a lifeline, I felt the presence of my mates. Their love, strength, and unwavering support wrapped around me, pulling me back to reality. Laz's calm reassurance, Samara's gentle encouragement, Orpheus's protective nature, and Silas's steady strength were all there, reminding me of who I was now. It was because of them that this power of mine had grown. Their love made me stronger.

I took a deep breath, grounding myself in their love. What I suffered through no longer felt like a weakness but a testament to my strength. Of what I had been able to endure in spite of him.

My father's expression shifted, the realization of what I had shown him sinking in. His eyes widened, and for the first time, I saw a flicker of understanding, maybe even regret.

With a final deep breath, I let the memories fade from his mind, pulling my newly expanded gift back into myself. I let my mind trace along the gift's edges, knowing there was more to it. I'd have time to explore it later.

I finally registered my mate's voices in my head, frantically checking in on me. They had felt my panic through the bond.

I'm okay. Thank you. I replied to my mates when I had regained my composure.

"What… what did you just do? I could see. I thought I saw…" Jacob asked, his eyes wide with concern. It was a strange look to see on his face. I didn't share this part of my history easily, not when I knew firsthand how some people reacted to it. And it was not a weapon I wanted to wield to hurt my father. My pain didn't need to be his, but all of a sudden, I wanted to share it. Not out of maliciousness but because it has made me who I am. Scars and all. It was the hardest thing I've ever had to survive, and I did it.

"That man abused me," I whispered.

He looked up at me, guilt and concern etched into his features. "Athena… He.. didn't.."

"He raped me," I admitted—the words like venom on my tongue.

My father's face twisted in agony, and I saw his body tremble. "No," he breathed, shaking his head. "No, I didn't know. I never knew. If I had…"

"He was a monster," I said, my voice breaking. "He took what didn't belong to him without regard for me or my mother. He hurt us both in ways neither of us have ever, or will ever truly heal from. He is the demon that haunts my nightmares. He is the violent creature I wish you could have protected me from."

He bowed his head, his shoulders shaking with silent sobs.

"I'm so sorry," he whispered over and over again, his voice melting with his cries into a soft cacophony of pain and regret. I stepped forward, kneeling before my father and gripping his chin to bring his eyes to mine.

"I don't need your guilt or your apologies," I said, not with venom but with strength and resolve. "I need you to hear me."

His tear-filled eyes met mine, and he nodded, the most broken I had ever seen him. In this light, he almost looked like me.

"When I was lost when I was broken… when that human piece of filth almost destroyed me…" He winced. "It was The Wanderers who taught me to love again. It was those gentle, beautiful, protective creatures out there who saved my life. They grabbed each broken shard of my heart and pieced me back together until I finally felt whole again. They are not monsters. They are my lifeline."

Tears slid down his face, the picture of a broken man whose very resolve was shaken to its core. I stood, suddenly feeling unable to face him like this.

I turned on a heel and sped from the room, rushing past the faces of my waiting mates and brother.

I could see from my mate's faces that they had heard the conversation with their exceptional hearing, but Archer looked at me with a hopeful expression.

"I need to get some air," I responded, feeling the twinge of panic return.

"What happened in there?" Archer asked eagerly.

"Just give me a second," I replied.

"Are you okay?" Laz asked, taking a tentative step forward. I nodded and took a deep breath.

"Yes, I just need to clear my head for a moment." I smiled shyly at them. I stepped toward the counter, plucking one of the pink roses from the vase. The aroma was so sweet and strong to my new senses that I instantly felt calmed. "I promise I'm okay. I just need a second. I'll be right back," I promised, taking the rose and heading toward the back door through the stacks of shelves. It would be safer to break down back there where no one could see me.

I stepped out the back door of the bookstore, the soft creak of the old wood blending with the sound of the ocean waves crashing against the pier below. The salty evening breeze greeted me. I twisted the stem of the delicate pink rose in my hand, letting the sting of the thorns pressing against my skin keep my mind from wandering too far into my memories.

The conversation with my father replayed in my mind like a storm of emotions swirling within me. I felt like I had finally broken through to him, made him see the pain and the truth. But the cost of dredging up those old memories was a weight I hadn't been prepared to carry again, and I needed a moment to process it all. Strange how that worked. Trauma. I could feel the safest and most secure I ever had, and still, those memories could sweep in and undo weeks, months, even of work.

I walked to the pier's edge, the wooden planks slightly damp beneath my feet. Staring out at the vast expanse of the dark ocean, I let myself feel the weight of everything. Tears blurred my vision as I looked down at the rose, the symbol of my new life, my new family. It was beautiful, but like the thorns, it also reminded me of the pain I had endured to get here.

My power was shifting and growing. I could feel it like a living thing inside my mind, expanding and evolving with each passing moment. I had shared my memories with someone else, letting them peek into my past. It was both exhilarating and terrifying. I took a deep breath, focusing on calming myself. But even still, it felt like there was more left to be discovered.

And then, out of nowhere, a sharp pain exploded at the back of my head. The world spun, and the rose slipped from my fingers, falling into the dark waters below. I barely had time to register what was happening before everything went black.

Darkness enveloped me, pulling me away from the pier, the ocean, the rose, and the memories of my father. My last conscious thought was a desperate hope that my mates would find me, that I wouldn't be lost to the darkness forever.

ORPHEUS

ELEVEN

How do you find someone who might be dead? Start at the scene of their supposed death, of course.

That's why I found myself stripped down to my undergarments and wading through the chilled water under the pier in the early morning. I'd left Athena in Samara's capable arms last night and instantly knew what I needed to do. I needed to find the bastard who attacked her. I needed to relieve the stress of this unknown variable from her life and from ours.

There was no sign of a body in these waters, but any signs of an escape may have washed away in the several weeks since it occurred. One thing was clear to me, though, if he had died, his body would have washed up on shore. This spot was too close to the beach, too public. No, he was alive. He was out there. Biding his time, I was sure of it. I knew predators. I spent most of my second life hunting them.

I made my way to the beach rental that he and Louis had secured and found old police lines. Of course, they'd searched the place and came up with nothing. I slipped in past the police tape and looked around. Both Greg and Louis had left their things behind, and there was no sign that he had returned for anything at all.

From there, I moved on to the motels in town, each one turning up nothing but dead ends and false leads.

As the evening wore on, and the moonlight bathed me in its glow, I felt my anxiety tightening around me like a vice. My thoughts kept drifting back to Athena, the image of her face, her eyes, and the fear that something terrible was happening to her, gnawing at my insides. I felt her panic a few minutes ago, powerful and raw. I wanted to alleviate the burden of some of her struggles even more. I had to find Greg before he chose to act.

Finally, I remembered my powers. I had been so focused on the physical search that I had neglected the tool that could, in theory, lead me straight to him. I silently cursed myself for getting so comfortable with the emotional silence Athena's mate bond had gifted me that I forgot to utilize one of the best weapons in my arsenal. Taking a deep breath, I closed my eyes, let my senses expand, and the switch flipped on. It was like trying to find the right radio station amid a sea of static. The emotions of the town's inhabitants swirled around me, now more overwhelming because of the start of the tourist season, a chaotic blend of everything from fear to excitement to sorrow and joy.

I tuned out the noise, focusing on a single thread, searching for the particular brand of malice that Greg exuded. It was difficult, almost overwhelming, but then I felt it– a sharp, vindictive emotion cutting through the background hum— hatred, nearly palpable in intensity, laced with a sickening sense of anticipation.

I locked onto it, following the thread through the maze of feelings around me. Greg's emotions were intense, burning with a dark satisfaction that chilled me to my core. I couldn't quite place his location. Too many other emotions were pricking at the edges of my consciousness to get that specific. He was planning something, and it was coming to fruition. A surge of fear and determination rushed through me, nearly knocking me off balance.

Without wasting another moment, I sprinted toward The Maine Plotline, toward Athena. She was there, and if he was going to act, it would be there. Panic and urgency drove me forward, my thoughts singularly focused on finding Athena before Greg could get to her. The sense of dread in my gut intensified with each step, but I couldn't let it slow me down.

As I ran, the faces, memories, and moments flashed before my eyes—Athena's laughter, strength, vulnerability. I had to find her, protect her. My heart pounded in my chest, and with every beat, the need to save her grew stronger.

I just hoped I wouldn't be too late.

Athena! I called out in my mind. But when no response came, I felt the pit of my stomach deepen. *Athena! Are you there?*

I tugged on the bond. Still there, still strong. But she didn't tug back.

I reached the front door and pounded on the glass, drawing the attention of the figures littered inside. I counted quickly. Athena wasn't there.

Laz barely had time to unlatch the door before I rushed inside.

"Where's Athena?" I asked, fury incarnate.

"Whoa, what's going on, Orpheus?" Samara asked, but I brushed past, looking around the stacks of books for my mate.

"Where is she?" I repeated, tossing open the office door, revealing Jacob Bennett. His eyes were red-rimmed from tears, and his shoulder and head slumped in defeat, but there was no sign of Athena.

"She stepped outside for a second," Silas responded, and I turned to glare at him, not bothering to shut the door to the office.

"And you let her go alone? With all the threats out there?" He looked like he wanted to fight back, but he saw the fear in my face, and his features softened.

"What happened?" He asked.

"I'll check the back," Archer said, bursting into action, heading toward the back of the shop.

"What's going on?" Jacob asked from inside the office, but I couldn't even focus enough to respond to him.

"Orpheus, breathe for a second," Samara said, touching my shoulders. I felt my breathing slow, but the panic didn't subside. "What is going on?"

"I felt Greg, I felt him. He's going to try something," I explained.

"Okay, okay," Samara replied, nodding as fear crossed her features.

I hear Archer's footsteps returning quickly, and the sinking feeling deepened. "She's gone," he croaked out.

The Wanderers devolved into a panic of epic proportions while I fell to my knees. Trying to focus on Greg's emotions again.

"Where the fuck are you?" I whispered.

I couldn't pinpoint it, not with how strongly my coven was feeling things. Their panic and anger overpowered the channels of my mind. I tried to push past their overwhelming reactions, but too much was happening, and too many feelings filled this small space for me to look beyond it. Then I felt a wave of guilt, so strong and so unlike any I'd felt before. My head snapped up to meet eyes with Jacob Bennett.

"Who the fuck took my daughter?" He asked fury in his words.

"A human," Archer spat back, running a hand through his hair.

Jacob damn near growled his response, his face etched with a desperation I hadn't known him to be capable of. His eyes, red-rimmed and hollow, pleaded with us. "I want to help find Athena," he said, his voice trembling with fear and anger. "Please, let me help."

'Absolutely fucking not," Silas exclaimed.

"Not a chance." Laz contributed while Samara scoffed her discontent.

"You're not going anywhere," Archer exclaimed.

Archer and my coven stood their ground, distrust, and anger radiating from them. Samara's eyes narrowed, and Silas's fists clenched at his sides. They weren't going to let him do a damn thing, not after everything he had done. But for some reason, I felt drawn to his emotions. I watched him, I felt the shift, something genuine and raw breaking through the surface.

I reached out with my power, feeling his emotions as if they were my own. Regret, guilt, and a newfound determination coursed through him. It was like a dam had broken, and he was finally seeing the consequences of his actions. Something Athena had said had gotten through to him, and he was seeing the other side of things for the first time. For the first time, he felt guilt.

"He's sincere," I said, rising from my knees and stepping forward. "She got through to him." I spoke with an edge of pride, and it felt almost euphoric, but the reminder of our current predicament quickly dispelled that feeling.

Jacob turned to me, tears welling in his eyes. "I know I've done terrible things to you. To all of you. And I am sorry for that." The room fell silent, the tension thick. I looked into his eyes, searching for any hint of deception. But all I saw and felt was a broken man, desperate to make amends. I searched his emotions for any sign of insincereity, but it wasn't there.

"She told me what you all did for her. How you saved her when she was drowning." His face twisted in anger again, and I felt the fury-filled hatred aimed at her stepfather. Jacob Bennett and I finally had something in common. "If you only let me do one last thing before you kill me, let me help bring her back."

For a moment, no one moved. Then, slowly, I nodded. "Alright," I said, feeling the weight of my decision. "You can help. But there won't be a second chance if you even consider betraying us."

Jacob nodded, a flicker of hope in his eyes, and his hope licked at the edges of my senses. "I understand. Thank you."

I stepped forward, intent to release his bindings, but Archer sidestepped into my path.

"Are you sure, Orpheus?" He asked. I studied the man before me. He looked so much like Athena and so much like the man bound to the chair just behind him, but he was also so incredibly individual. The pain in his eyes was unique to him.

His emotions were tumultuous. Anger and disappointment were at the forefront, but a tendril of wild hope danced around. He so desperately wished for his father to have changed, for him to finally see the right side of things.

"I can't say with any ounce of certainty that he won't hate vampires for the rest of his life," I said, glancing over Archer's shoulders at the broken man. "But he loves Athena, you can't fake that. He will help us find her."

"We don't need his help," Silas argued. "We can take down a puny human. Hell, she can take him down herself now, too."

I felt Laz and Samara's silent agreement in their emotions.

"What if we run into Galvin? We may need his expertise. He may be the only edge we have." I nodded to Jacob.

"I hope you're right," Archer whispered, stepping to the side and out of my path. I moved forward, ready to release the man who had tortured us. The man who had killed Alora. The man who had been the source of our turmoil for years.

The man who had given life to my mate.

"I hope I am, too," I replied and sliced through the ropes at his wrists.

ATHENA

TWELVE

I woke up slowly, instantly feeling a table's cold, hard surface beneath me. My arms and legs were bound, but as I looked around, I quickly assessed the situation. I felt tired but not weak. I did have a massive headache stemming from where I was hit, and the throbbing pain was enough to keep me from establishing the mental link with my mates, but I could feel my supernatural healing already starting to take effect. I'd keep trying to reach them until I could get through. The bindings were simple ropes– nothing that could hold me if I decided to break free. My captor had no idea what I was and just how little these bindings could hold me and that mistake would cost him.

The dim light filtering through a small window high on the wall cast eerie shadows across the space. An old fishing warehouse, I determined by the smell of rotten fish and the sound of the waves so nearby. My senses sharpened as I took in the musty scent of old wood and metal, the faint sound of wood creaking somewhere nearby. There was no one in sight, but I knew better than to assume I was alone.

As I tugged experimentally at the ropes, I confirmed what I had suspected there was nothing here made to hinder my vampiric abilities. No Hunter tricks, no special restraints. This wasn't the work of the Nameless Hunters or Doctor Kline Galvin. This was Greg.

A cold fury settled in my chest. He thought he had me right where he wanted, but he had no idea just how wrong he was. I could easily rip through these bindings and disappear into the night, but he'd still be out there, still planning something to hurt me. I allowed myself to relax on the table, deciding to wait. Let him think he had the upper hand. Let him come to me.

The seconds ticked by, each one feeling like an eternity. My thoughts drifted to my mates, my friends, and my brother. I knew they would be searching for me, but I was on my own for now. And that was just fine. I could handle Greg. I smiled at just how true that statement felt.

I turned and saw a phone sitting atop a tripod facing me. There was no indication that it was on, but I made a mental note to be careful about overtly using my abilities in front of it.

I listened intently, focusing on the faintest of sounds. The creak of a door opening somewhere in the building. The soft shuffle of footsteps. He was coming. My muscles tensed, ready to spring into action. The waiting was almost over, and soon, Greg would learn just how big a mistake he had made.

Greg burst into the room, his face twisted in a mask of anger and frustration. The moonlight gleamed off his sweaty forehead. His eyes were wild, darting between the phone and me with a volatile mix of rage and desperation.

"Athena Landry," he spoke, his voice nearly unrecognizable, maybe on purpose to avoid his voice being identifiable on the camera.

"Gregory Holden," I replied, letting a soft smile play on my lips. His lips turned up in a snarl.

"Don't say my name, you fucking bitch," he snapped.

"Why not, Gregory Holden?" I taunted. He growled, nearly stepping into the camera's frame, but paused and took a breath.

"You're trying to piss me off, so you can justify killing me like you did with Louis," he claimed.

I narrowed my eyes at him.

"Not that I want a reason for anything like that, but you did kidnap me…so.."

"Shut the fuck up!" he interjected.

I shrugged, trying to show just how indifferent I was. I had been in positions like this far too many times in my life, but for the first time, I felt like I had all the power. It was intoxicating. This man had once terrified me, but now I pitied him.

"Why won't you just admit it?" He roared, his voice echoing off the metal walls of the warehouse. "Why won't you confess to what you and your fucking harem did to Louis? I know you're involved. I know you all are!"

I remained still, my gaze steady and defiant. The ropes binding me were a mere inconvenience, a temporary hold that I had no intention of letting him know I could easily escape from. Instead, I leaned my head back against the table, feigning nonchalance. My heart was calm, even as his rage intensified.

"I told you before, Gregory Holden. Your 'friend' tried to rape me, and my partners pulled him off of me and sent him on his way." On his way to hell, but he didn't need to know that part.

"No, he didn't, you fucking slut!" I felt the bubble of anger slip through my calm exterior. I had been called my fair share of names, such as that, when the town first heard about what my stepfather did to me. They affected me greatly at the time, but now they stung me differently.

"Don't call me that," I warned. "Louis was a rapist and an asshole who drugged me because he couldn't get what he wanted from me. My mates sent him on his way… and if he never returns to Shockgrove, it would be a better place."

Greg's face flushed a deep, angry red. He stormed over to the phone and slapped it, making it jolt. "Don't play games with me, Athena! This is your last chance to come clean. I know you killed him, and you're going to confess."

I could see the steam practically pouring out of his ears. It was clear he was expecting me to crack, to break under the pressure of his accusations. Of the bindings that he secured around me. But I refused to give him the satisfaction. I met his gaze with an unyielding calmness, a smirk tugging at the corner of my lips.

"I'm not afraid of you."

I was surprised by just how much truth was in that statement.

Greg's fury seemed to reach a boiling point. He kicked the tripod, sending the phone toppling to the ground. I had no idea if it was still recording, but the lens was faced down. His eyes narrowed, and he marched over to me, grabbing a fistful of my shirt and shaking me violently. The ropes tightened painfully around my wrists, but I remained silent, not giving him the reaction he was so desperate for.

"You're not afraid because you're arrogant," Greg spat, his breath hot and furious. "But you will be. You'll confess, or I'll make you wish you had."

Despite his threats, I stayed calm, forcing myself to breathe steadily, even though his hands burned into my skin. My mind was already working on the escape plan. Greg's temper was his greatest weapon, and it was also his greatest weakness. The more he raged, the more control I had. I wasn't playing the victim, and I wasn't submitting. And that, more than anything, seemed to enrage him further.

"You're a fucking whore. You can't say Louis tried to rape you and then spread your legs for four fucking people at the same time," he growled in my face. His hand slipped into the waistband of his jeans, and for a brief moment, I feared that he might try to replicate Louis' attempt, but there was no lust in his gaze. It was only fury. His hand returned with a knife this time, and on instinct, my body tensed with fear. He must have seen it because he smiled wickedly, stepping closer.

"I told you you'd be afraid, slut," he whispered into my ear, pressing the knife against my throat.

I'd reached my breaking point. Ripping through the bindings at my wrists, I felt myself cry out in anger, in fury, in contempt for all the times people underestimated me, every time they tried to break me down or chip away pieces of me until there was nothing left. I moved too quickly for Greg to even comprehend. The knife bit into my skin only slightly, but once my hands were free, I twisted it from his grasp. My arms barred around his throat from behind, and I pressed the knife against his neck this time. "And I told you not to call me that," I growled into his ear.

"What the…" he stuttered, shock in his tone.

"I'll give you one chance. Get the fuck out of this town. Take your fucking vendetta with you and leave me alone," I asserted, feeling every ounce of strength in my soul.

My headache began to subside just in time to hear my mate's worried and frantic calls. Just as I prepared to respond, to ensure them I was safe, I felt their presence as they busted into the space. Their eyes searching frantically for me, their forms nearly shifted, but just human enough not to alert Greg to their nature.

Trailing behind them was Archer, who looked terrified. And then, surprising me entirely, was my father. His form took up the rear of the group, he stood tall and menacingly, prepared for a fight, but my mates weren't registering him as a threat to them. What did that mean?

"Athena!" Orpheus' voice was a mix of relief and surprise as my Wanderers rushed forward. Relief was evident on their faces.

I turned to them, my heart pounding. "You came."

Greg's face twisted in confusion and anger. "What the hell is this?"

Jacob, my father, stepped forward, his face a mask of fury. Before Greg could react, his fist connected with his jaw, sending him reeling. "That's for hurting my daughter, you piece of scum," he spat.

Archer moved swiftly, taking over and securing Greg, his eyes flashing with barely restrained rage. I turned from Greg, finally feeling able to let my guard down, and fell into the embrace of my mates. Their arms wrapped around me, grounding me, and for a moment, I felt safe amidst the chaos.

"Thank you," I whispered, my voice breaking. "Thank you for coming."

Orpheus gripped my face in his palms, his eyes searching mine. "Are you okay?"

I nodded. "I had it under control," I admitted, loving how that truth made me feel.

"Of course you did," Samara added proudly. Archer handed off a dazed Greg to Silas and embraced me. My gaze shifted to our father. He stood a little apart from the group, watching me interact with my mates with an intensity that made my breath catch. I moved towards him, Archer's hand secured in mine, my voice low so Greg couldn't hear from where he stood, thrashing in Silas' hold. "You came to save me? With them?"

Jacob's eyes softened, and he nodded. "Saving you was the only thing that mattered to me, Athena. You are both more important to me than anything. I'm sorry it took me this long to see it. I've fucked up. A lot. And I'd like to make up for it if you let me."

I glanced over at Archer. Jacob had abandoned me, but he had let someone hurt Archer, ordered it, in fact. How could you come back from something like that?

"Fucked up is putting it lightly," Archer hissed.

"I know," Jacob replied, hanging his head.

"But for Athena's sake," Archer said as he glanced at me. "I'll give you the chance to earn my forgiveness."

I felt a slight moment of hope blossom between the three of us. We'd never have a relationship like the one I used to dream about, but maybe we'd have something different. Something more… us.

"Thank you, both of you."

Just as he finished speaking, he suddenly recoiled, his face contorting in pain. I couldn't move. I couldn't even breathe. He stumbled forward, doubling over at the waist. That's when I saw it, the arrow lodged deeply in his back, piercing his heart. "No!" I cried out, the sound ripping from my throat as I rushed forward to him, catching him before he fell. Archer joined me, our father collapsing into our arms. We settled him onto the ground, my eyes unable to look away from the arrow.

My heart was in my mouth, terror and pain overwhelming me as I held my father. "No, no, no," I whispered, tears streaming down my face.

The others were already reacting, their eyes scanning the area for the threat. But all I could focus on was my father, his blood staining my hands as I tried to keep him upright. "Dad, stay with me," Archer pleaded, his voice trembling.

"Where the fuck did that come from?" Silas growled, holding tightly to a thrashing Greg.

"Keep your eyes peeled," Orpheus commanded angrily.

"Samara, please!" I cried out, my throat raw as I screamed. The blood on my hands was thick and warm, and I didn't even notice the hunger over the fear. She rushed over, but before she could place her hands on my father, another arrow emerged from the darkness and slammed into Greg's throat. Silas jolted, his face wide as he saw just how close it had come to hitting him. Greg's steps faltered, and he pressed a hand against his throat. Dark blood spilled from the wound as he fell to his knees.

"Don't even think about it," a sinister voice whispered from the darkness. The sound sent an eerie chill down my spine. And that's when I heard it, a loud, high-pitched ringing. I pressed my hands against my ears, trying to drown out the offending noise, but it persisted. I felt the power within me slip away as if it was retreating from the noise. My mates spun, putting their backs to each other, each straining painfully from the noise.

"What's going on?" Archer asked frantically, watching me shake my head in pain.

Samara focused her gaze on my father, a frustrated grunt coming from her. "He's blocking our gifts. I can't heal him."

"No, no, no," Archer spat. "Please, stay with me."

"I'm.. so sorry. Both of you," he sputtered, and I felt my dead heart crack. "I love…"

The light drifted from his eyes, and I knew that without Samara's healing abilities, he would be gone soon.

The air felt charged. This was it. I could feel it. The moment that either vampires or Hunters emerge victorious. There would be no draw. Two were walking in, and only one could walk out. I squeezed my father's hand, knowing that the only way to save him would be to win, and stood.

My father's blood dripped from my coated hands down my arms as I let the shift take over. My vision reddened, and my claws and fangs elongated. I lifted one arm and tracked my tongue from elbow to wrist, letting the jolt of fresh-from-the-vein human blood spur my strength. I felt my mates prepare, joining me in a formation. We were about to take on *the* Hunter himself. And if I had anything to say about it, we were going to fucking win.

ORPHEUS

THIRTEEN

Why the fuck did I turn it off? I scolded myself. The moment I found my mate, I had to flip it all off because the relief and the anger were all too much, and all I wanted to feel was her and her alone. So I turned it off. I let the emotional radar quiet in my mind, and because of that, I missed the Hunter-sized threat heading directly for us.

I let my guard down, and we were ambushed.

And if we lost anyone here tonight, it would be my fault.

I tried to switch it on now as the eerie voice bounced through the warehouse, but whatever device he had was dulling our senses… leveling the playing field. Hunters had been fighting against vampires for centuries, finding ways to use our advantages against us. I shouldn't be surprised that Galvin brought a little toy like this.

Amidst the panic and anger of my own emotions, I felt the tingle of familiarity claw at my mind. The voice echoing through the chamber gnawed at me. I don't recall running into him at the headquarters during either of our ventures there, but for some reason, his voice sent a wave of recognition over me. But I couldn't place it.

The scent of blood was thick in the room as both Greg and Jacob Bennett bled out on the floor at our feet. Archer was pressing his hands onto Jacob's form, trying to staunch the worst of the bleeding. Greg was dead. I heard the last pump of his heart only moments ago, and now he was gone. I couldn't say I was distraught that the man who injured, stalked, threatened, and kidnapped my mate was dead, but I didn't want the Hunters to be the ones who rid the world of him.

"Hello, Kline," I said to the void of darkness. My senses were dulled by the device emitting the high-pitched screech, so I couldn't tell where exactly he was. It almost felt like he was everywhere.

"Orpheus," the voice whispered in a hiss. "I wish I could say it's nice seeing you again."

I tried to hide my confusion from my face. "Sorry, I don't recall us ever meeting. Perhaps you didn't make much of an impression," I replied tauntingly. Silas was at my back, and Laz and Samara were standing to my side with their shoulders pressed together. Athena stood near Jacob Bennett, and my eyes kept glancing at her to ensure she was okay. Her form had fully shifted. She was stunning. Her vampiric features were hauntingly terrifying, with a beauty only she could possess. Still, I didn't enjoy the reason for her shift.

The voice chuckled in response, sending an eerie chill down my spine. Why the hell was he able to affect me like this? I shook my head, trying not to let the nagging feeling get to me.

"You have grown a spine since last we met." Then, finally, stepping out of the shadows was Doctor Kline Galvin. The doctor stood before us, his figure cloaked in the Nameless Hunters' familiar yet unnerving white mask. His body was strong and built, every muscle seemingly coiled and ready to strike. His stance was firm, exuding an aura of confidence that made the air feel heavier. He was not a man to be underestimated, and his presence alone was enough to send a shiver to my extremities.

From behind the mask, his eyes were cold and calculating, scanning the room with a predator's gaze. There was something about him that tugged at my subconscious. The sensation was like an itch I couldn't scratch, growing more insistent with every second that ticked by.

But for the life of me, I couldn't place him. His identity remained just out of reach, hidden behind the mask.

As he stalked forward, I glanced around, sure that he wouldn't come alone to fight us. He must have backup here somewhere, and I wouldn't let him distract us from that threat.

"We need to be vigilant. There has to be others," I whispered under my breath so the Doctor couldn't hear me. My coven was on edge, ready to spring into action at a moment's notice, but we remained still, poised for the attack we knew was coming.

He lifted his crossbow and took aim at none other than Jacob Bennett. "Bennett, Bennett, Bennett," he mused disappointedly. "You know what we must do to traitors, don't you?" Archer stood, placing himself between the arrow and his father. "Ah, Archer, right? I knew I saw weakness in your eyes that day. I'd hoped I was wrong. But it seems you got your backbone from your father." With Samara's ability hindered, if Archer took a hit, we might lose him too. I couldn't watch Athena lose both of them tonight. I took a menacing step forward, and Galvin aimed at me.

"I'm done following your lead, Galvin. What you're doing isn't right," Jacob seethed through gritted teeth.

"Is that so?" He tilted his masked head, and I almost felt the wicked smirk.

"I won't let you hurt my family," Jacob sputtered, blood spilling from his mouth. Archer's pain was so evident on his face I didn't need my gift to feel it. He knew, as we all did, that Jacob wouldn't survive without healing.

"I forgot the part where I said I cared what you thought," Galvin mused before aiming his crossbow again. He moved so fast that even I couldn't see it until the arrow flew through the air. I tried to move and call for Archer, but the arrow found its target—lodging in Jacob's neck. A violent sob ripped from Archer and Athena's throats. It was a cry of pain, of anger. Of loss.

The briefest image of Alora with a stake in her heart flashed in my mind.

"Dad! Please! No!" Archer cried, but it was too late. Jacob was gone.

Athena readied herself to rush toward Galvin, but Silas placed a hand on her shoulder, keeping her back.

"Why don't we make this interesting?" Galvin said as he gripped a remote from his pocket. Pressing the button, he sent out another wave of that ear-splitting screech. The moment the sound intensified, it felt like a knife slicing through my senses. My head throbbed, and my vision wavered as I tried desperately to focus on the threat before us. I felt my strength falter and my hearing deafen. He had the upper hand, and that fucking pissed me off. He stood there, a crossbow in hand, arrows at the ready, the pointed tips glistening in the soft light of the warehouse.

Then he attacked.

Every arrow he loosed flew with impossible speed and precision, soaring toward its mark with deadly accuracy. The first struck Archer in the leg, and he fell to his knees with a cry of pain. Athena quickly rushed to move him behind a stack of crates, the only cover we could find in the chaos of the warehouse. He cried out and clawed out for his father, but Athena pried him away and got him to a fraction of safety despite his protests.

The high-pitched device was crippling us. Our enhanced senses, strength, and speed were all dulled, and we were barely more than human. Once her brother was safely tucked behind the cover, Athena's eyes darted around, trying to pinpoint the source of the sound. Silas and Laz were already strategizing, their minds racing even through the pain.

"We need to find that device and shut it down," Silas hissed, his voice strained. "We won't stand a chance against him otherwise."

I nodded, pushing through the agony. "I'll draw his fire. Laz, can you track the source?"

Laz, despite the grimace on their face, gave a determined nod. "I'll do my best."

With a deep breath, I dashed out from behind the crates, making myself a moving target. Galvin's eyes followed me, another arrow already knocked and ready. I dodged, trying to make it difficult for him to get a clear shot, but my speed was hindered. An arrow whizzed past my ear, so close I could feel the air shift.

"Come on, you bastard," I muttered under my breath. "Keep your eyes on me."

Laz was moving, too, their eyes scanning the rafters and corners of the warehouse. Another arrow flew, grazing my arm, but I kept moving, the pain secondary to the mission at hand.

"There!" Laz shouted, pointing to a small device mounted on the upper level of this warehouse. How long had he been planning this? Did we walk directly into his trap? How did he know Greg planned to pick this location? "It's up there!"

Athena's eyes met mine, a silent understanding passing between us. She was still weakened by the sound as we all were, but she gathered her strength, her determination glistening in her red eyes. "Silas, give me a boost."

Silas positioned himself under the catwalk of the upper level and cupped his hands together. Athena stepped into them, and he launched her upward with all the strength he could muster despite the stinging pain. She caught the catwalk's railing, her fingers gripping tightly as she swung herself up.

Galvin's attention snapped to her, but before he could react by sending an arrow, I hurled a heavy crate in his direction, forcing him to dodge. It bought Athena the precious seconds she needed.

She reached the device, her fingers working quickly. The sound intensified momentarily, a final burst of agony, and then– silence. Blessed silence. The relief was immediate as our senses sharpened, strength returned, and the fog lifted from our minds.

Athena dropped back down, landing lightly beside me. "That's much better." She stretched her neck, shaking off the last remnants of pain.

Galvin's eyes narrowed, realizing his advantage was gone. "You think this changes anything?" he snarled.

But it did change everything. With our full powers restored, we were ready. He let a few more arrows fly in quick succession, but we were able to easily dodge them as we made our way to his side of the warehouse, where he had remained in relative safety until now.

"Holy shit," Laz exclaimed next to me, and I turned to see their face just as an arrow pierced my shoulder. I hissed, quickly pushing Laz behind the crates and evading another lethal blow.

"What is it?" I asked through gritted teeth. The pain was sharp, and I felt the toxic tip slowly seep into my blood system. I reached up, ripping the arrow from my skin, gritting my teeth at the pain as it pulled through my tender skin, but instantly felt the toxin stop its maddening dissolvement.

"I can feel his blood," Laz said, their eyes glassy and wide.

"What do you feel?" I asked as Silas tossed another crate at Galvin, which crashed against the wall. I looked over and saw Samara was focused on healing Archer's wounds. Archer was pale empty, his eyes unfocused and glistening with tears.

"He's not human, Orpheus," Laz said finally, and my head snapped to face them. Shocked.

"What do you mean, he's not human?" I asked in a hushed whisper as another round of arrows lodged in the crates behind which we were hidden.

"I can feel the venom in his blood. He's a vampire, Orpheus. He's one of us." Laz whispered it, but if what they said was true, it was loud enough for Galvin to hear. The barrage of arrows slowed, and I heard the man sigh.

"A vampire," I said quietly, knowing he heard me. If he was, in fact, one of us, it meant he could hear everything the same as I could. "You're a vampire who hunts vampires…" I was still trying to wrap my mind around it when I stood from behind the crates to look him in his fucking traitorous eyes.

He tilted his head slightly as if considering whether to answer. Then, with a chilling calmness, he spoke. "You really don't remember me, do you? Perhaps I can help jog your memory."

With deliberate slowness, he reached up and removed the mask, revealing a face that sent a jolt of recognition through me, ripping through the recesses of my lost memories and tearing a piece of them free. The features were exactly the same as they had been all those years ago but held a more menacing glow, and there was no mistaking the man who had haunted my nightmares until his visage disappeared into the lost memories of my human life.

The one who had turned me.

Realization crashed over me like a tidal wave, leaving me reeling. "You," I whispered, the word laced with a mixture of shock and anger.

"Me," he replied, a cruel smile curling at the edges of his lips. "It's been a long time, hasn't it? And now, it seems, our paths have crossed once more."

The tension in the room ratcheted up a notch, and I could feel my mate's concern through our bond. The Wanderers were coiled like snakes, ready to strike at the right moment. They were prepared to fight, ready to protect, but they also sensed the personal nature of this encounter and gave me this moment to confront the phantom of my history alone.

"Who is he, Orpheus?" Samara asked.

"My sire," I whispered, my eyes locked on his figure as the blurry memory of his face clarified in my mind.

"You're a hypocrite," Athena hissed, and Galvin sighed.

"I'm a Hunter," he replied.

"How can you hate what you are?" Silas demanded. "Why kill your own kind?"

"I simply admitted to myself what our kind has shied away from for centuries… we are monsters, and this Earth would be better off without us tainting its soils with our unnatural existence."

I'd heard that kind of radicalized speech before from Hunters or humans with unfortunate knowledge of our supernatural existence. Still, I'd never heard that kind of violent diatribe from a member of our own community.

"One day, I woke up from my blood-hazed stupor of murder, bloodlust, and violence and saw what I had become. I was disgusted when I saw who I was and what I had done. I knew then that my purpose in life was to eradicate every last one of us from this plane of existence… and when my task is finished, I will follow to the fiery pits of hell where we belong." His eyes darkened into the signature red as he spoke.

"Why turn me? Why make more vampires if you're trying to eradicate us?" I spat at him. Disgust and anger colored my tone.

He sighed. "Because I was no match against some of the more powerful of our kind. Not when they'd been gifted their unique and unnatural abilities." He spat the word unnatural like a slur. "Myself? I wasn't gifted any abilities in my new existence. At least, I didn't think I was. But when I created my first heir, I realized that when he matured and developed his gift. I was able to siphon it for myself."

"You made me an heir?" I whispered, putting the pieces together. Heirs were different than turned vampires, they required a more detailed turning ritual, and the benefit was a blood tie that lasted as long as they lived. I glared at the man in front of me. Disgust blooming in my chest. How could I be tied to a monster like him?

"Don't feel so surprised, Orpheus," he taunted, hinting at his ability to feel my emotions. I growled, my chest vibrating. "I made vampires, so I could finally build an arsenal of powers to use against the very vampires I created."

"How many," Samara asked, her voice quivering.

"How many heirs have I created? Or how many have I killed?" He clarified with a wicked smirk.

"You bastard," Silas tossed out.

We weren't acting or rushing forward because my coven had likely put together the same thing I had. If this man was the vampire who turned me, he was ancient. His strength was undoubtedly unmatched by any of us. And if he was telling the truth about his ability, he may have powers unlike any we've ever seen running through his veins.

Somehow, he'd managed to outnumber us all on his own.

"So," he began. "My sired…" he whispered softly, sending a wicked shiver down my spine. "It's time for you to be sent to where you belong. I will win, and you will die. You can fight if you'd like. But this ends today. The Wanderers will die tonight."

I glanced at my coven. Their eyes met mine with the same burning intensity I felt reflected in my own heart. We had so much to fight for and live for, and we were not going to go down without a fight.

I clenched my fists and let the shift take over completely.

"You're going to regret the day you created me," I promised before rushing forward into a losing battle.

LAZ

FOURTEEN

Galvin moved with inhuman speed. His every step was a blur as we squared against him. I still hadn't shaken off the shock that hit me when I felt his blood and noticed the vampiric venom that danced within. We rushed forward, but my chest tightened because I knew we were going up against someone with an arsenal of abilities we'd stand no chance against. But we were going to try.

Our bodies clashed in a flurry of blows and claws, but Galvin managed to stave off the worst of our attacks with ease. Our speed was entirely unmatched by his. Galvin chuckled darkly, offering me a vicious smirk.

One moment, we were standing on solid ground, and in the next, everything shifted. The warehouse walls twisted and stretched, the floor beneath us undulating like the surface of a stormy sea. It was disorienting and terrifying. The image was so believable that I had to focus hard to keep my balance. The air seemed to hum with his power, and I could see my friends struggling to adjust to the new reality he had painted for us in our minds.

"It's not real!" I screamed out.

Galvin laughed, his form flickering as if he himself were made of shadows.

"Maybe not, but this is," he taunted as he waved a hand, and the floor beneath us turned into quicksand. My feet sank immediately, the thick, heavy sand pulling me down. Silas and Orpheus were similarly trapped. Their movements slowed as they tried to free themselves. Samara and Athena, light on their feet managed to dodge the space barely.

Panic surged through me. We would be at his mercy if we didn't counter this quickly. I closed my eyes, reaching out with my power. I focused on the nearly liquified ground beneath us, willing it to solidify. The sand resisted, considering it wasn't my common medium, but I pushed harder, my control over the contents of the mixture at my feet, fighting for dominance over Galvin's control of our minds.

Slowly, agonizingly, the quicksand began to solidify. I could feel the resistance of Galvin's power, a dark, malevolent force pushing back against me. But I persisted. I wouldn't let him win. With a final, concentrated effort, the ground beneath us hardened, turning back into solid earth, allowing us just enough time to distance ourselves from the depths of Galvin's abilities.

"Move!" I yelled, urging my friends to take advantage of the brief respite.

Silas charged forward, his strength and anger renewed. Orpheus followed, his eyes glowing with predatory fury. I couldn't imagine being told that I was sired by an evil man like this, let alone his heir. Athena moved with deadly grace, her blood-covered claws gleaming as she struck at Galvin. I focused on the air around us, trying to make sense of the lingering effects of his reality warping. What was real, and what wasn't?

With a flick of his wrist, Galvin summoned a torrent of water from seemingly nowhere. The liquid swirled and formed razor-sharp blades that sliced through the air. Samara barely managed to deflect one of the blades, her healing powers working overtime to mend the shallow cuts it left behind on her skin.

Orpheus lunged at Galvin, his fangs bared, but Galvin was ready. He conjured a wall of flame that forced Orpheus to retreat, the heat searing his skin. He screamed out, clutching at his arm. Athena tried to take advantage of the distraction, her claws aimed at Galvin's heart, but he vanished in a puff of smoke, reappearing behind her with a mocking smile.

"Is this the best you can do?" he taunted, his voice echoing around us.

The frustration and fear in my coven was palpable. We were outmatched, and Galvin knew it. He was toying with us, using his numerous gifts to keep us on the defensive.

Silas lunged forward, managing to land a blow across Glavin's chest. He grunted in pain and recoiled, but Galvin whispered something unintelligible before Silas could manage another hit. Silas's whole body froze, his muscles bulging from the effort.

"Silas!" I heard Athena cry out.

Slowly, my friend turned to face us, his body rigid and tense. His eyes were red and feral as they scanned over us as if he were looking at us for the first time.

"Silas?" I asked, not recognizing the look in his eyes or the way he tracked us like prey.

"Well, what are you waiting for?" Galvin said, and before I could react, Silas lunged again. This time at me. His claws dug into my shoulder, and I screamed out as pain radiated down my arm.

"Silas, what the hell?" I grunted, pressing my hand against the wound.

He didn't reply, but I don't think he could have even if he wanted to. There was an almost wicked haze over his eyes as he glared at me. Galvin had done something to him. He was controlling him somehow. Silas growled at me, drawing my attention back to him. His eyes were vacant, his expression blank and glazed. I knew it wasn't him, it was Galvin's twisted control that had taken over, but it hurt more than I cared to admit to see him looking at me like that. When he lunged, it was with all the power and ferocity I had come to love about him, but now it was turned against us.

"Silas, please!" Athena cried out, desperation tinging her voice as Silas lashed out again. I tried to fend him off without causing him harm, but he was too strong, too relentless.

Orpheus and Samara moved in tandem to get to me. Their efforts were a coordinated dance to subdue our friend without hurting him. But his blows were powerful, and one struck my lower abdomen, sending a searing pain through me. I staggered back, clutching the wound, blood trickling between my fingers.

"Silas!" Athena pleaded, tears in her eyes as she sprinted toward the trashing Silas. She tried to reach him, to break through the fog of Galvin's control, but it was like shouting into the wind. He was deaf to our cries. Orpheus and I gripped each arm while Samara tossed her arms around his neck and held him barred.

We struggled to hold him, our muscles straining under his violent strength. "We need to do something," Orpheus grunted, barely managing to keep Silas's arm from breaking free.

Athena stepped forward, determination etched on her face. "Hold him still," she commanded. I tightened our grip on Silas, my heart heavy with the knowledge that we might have to hurt him to save him.

She reached up and placed her hands on Silas's face, her fingers trembling. He tried to pull back, grunting, but she did not relent. "Silas, come back to us," she whispered, her voice filled with raw emotion.

For a moment, nothing happened. Then, Athena's eyes flashed gold, a brilliant, otherworldly light. My breath caught in my throat. I'd never seen anything like that before. It was beautiful. Perhaps even more shocking then was that as Silas' eyes met Athena's, they mirrored that same golden flash. There was a tense silence as the glow enveloped them both, and I could feel the power dance in the air.

Slowly, Silas's body began to relax. His struggles ceased, and his eyes cleared, the golden light fading. He blinked, confusion giving way to recognition. "Athena…" he murmured, his voice hoarse.

We released him, and he stumbled into Athena's arms, clutching her like a lifeline. "I'm so sorry," he whispered, flicking his eyes to me, his voice breaking. Athena held him tightly, her tears mingling with his.

"It's okay," she soothed, her fingers brushing through his hair. I nodded my agreement. "You're back with us now. That's all that matters."

"How touching," Galvin teased. "Have you realized that I cannot and will not be beaten yet?" As he raised his hand again, the air around us seemed to thicken, turning into a suffocating fog that choked the breath from our lungs.

The fog seeped through my nose, burning my lungs as it enveloped my senses. I doubled over, coughing out the offending fog, but the more I tried to dissolve the toxin in the mist, the more it poured in.

I fell to my knees, my body tired, my power weak in the face of Galvin and his overwhelming abilities. No wonder Nameless had survived for this long. This vampire was damn near invincible.

I felt the bond in my chest vibrate with panic. Athena's fear gripped and pulled at the thread of our connection. She was desperate to reach us.

He's too strong. She cried into our minds, her physical voice far too injured by the fog to say anything out loud.

We can't give up. Samara.

We need something big. Silas.

"Vampires are the devil's mistake, and I will not stop until every last one of us is rotting in hell," Galvin seethed, his voice thick with rage and fury.

Just as I expected the fog to drown me, a deafening crunch permeated the space, and the fog immediately dissipated. I jumped to my feet quickly, ready to fight whatever Galvin had planned for us next. He was cradling his head, his venomous blood pouring from his ear, where a hatchet was buried into his temple. I glanced around in shock, and that's when I saw them.

Bursting through the warehouse door, pouring in through the open windows, and slipping in from the shadows were dozens of vampires. Some faces I'd recognized from our brief meetings in passing, some I'd never seen before. But they all had one thing in common. Their faces, bodies, and souls each carried scars dealt to them by the one man now standing alone in the middle of us all.

These vampires, these survivors, once scattered and afraid, were now united with a single purpose. To reclaim their lives and their freedom and take down Nameless once and for all.

A familiar older woman led the survivors, her long black locs swinging as she moved with a grace that commanded respect. Her skin was deep ebony, and her eyes burned with fierce determination. She raised her hand, and the vampires behind her surged forward, a wave of vengeance and hope. I recognized her gentle features from when we met her in New Orleans when she gifted us the ability to walk in the sunlight.

"We meet again," she said in her comforting, thick cajun accent, nodding toward Orpheus.

"Zula, you got my message," Orpheus said, relief flooding his voice.

"We all did," she nodded to the menacing crowd of furious vampires around.

"He's a vampire," Orpheus warned. Zula nodded.

"Of course he is," she hissed.

"You think backup is enough to stop me?" Galvin seethed, pulling the hatchet from his head and letting the blood pour from the wound. "You only saved me the trouble of tracking every last one of you *monsters* down!" He cried out, his features shifting feral. "I look forward to delivering you all to your deaths." He said before he struck out again. But this time, the vampires descended on him.

The air was thick with the scent of blood and the metallic tang of fear as we fought against Galvin. They were a sight to behold. Vampires who had been in hiding for years and hunted relentlessly by the Nameless Hunters. Their eyes gleamed with determination and a fierce desire for vengeance.

I could see the desperation in Galvin's feral eyes. He summoned shadows to obscure his movements and conjured fire to burn us, but we were relentless. He had to fight off blow after blow as dozens of vampires swarmed him. We fought with a ferocity born of years of anger and fear. We wanted their freedom, and we were willing to die for it.

Despite our new numbers, Galvin's ancient and overwhelming powers still gave him the upper hand. He moved quickly, striking out with deadly precision, sending several of our reinforcements scattering across the floor, blood pouring from them.

But he was also growing nervous. The constant barrage from all sides was wearing him down. He couldn't keep this up forever. We just needed to survive long enough to weaken him.

Just then, an idea so big and impossible formed in my mind. It was crazy and wild enough that it might actually work.

"Orpheus," I called out, rushing over to him. He glanced over at me, and I saw his face. Blood smeared across his features, and already violent bruises bloomed on his cheeks. "I have an idea," I rushed hurriedly.

"What is it?" He asked. I turned my gaze to Galvin, who fought off the barrage of attacks, but only barely, and let my power wash over him.

His blood pumped violently in his body as a result of his exertion. I let my power dance through the veins under his skin, feeling the venom pulsing within it. The venom that created this monster. The venom that made him one of us. The venom that gave him immortality.

The venom that I was going to remove.

"We will never defeat him like this," I admitted, and Orpheus's angry face only confirmed the truth I already knew. "But what if he was mortal…" I whispered and saw the recognition flash on his face.

"You think you could?" He asked, incredulously but hopefully.

I let the power take hold of the venom, analyzing it until I felt every ounce of it within his bloodstream. It was so thoroughly intertwined with the human blood that remained in his body that it took me a while to find the edges of it all. To identify the pieces of him that were mortal versus what was this supernatural amalgamation before us. My head began to ache as I pressed against the very edge of my power. I closed my eyes and strained.

What's going on? Athena's voice in my mind called out.

Laz has an idea. Orpheus responded for me.

I was thankful because I couldn't do anything other than focus on the edges of the venom, tracing out each ounce of it.

What idea? Athena prodded.

They're going to make him mortal. Orpheus said his confidence was supportive but perhaps too premature. I felt blood trickle from my nose as my head throbbed.

They're in pain. I can feel their injuries. Samara cried out.

They're going to push too far. Silas responded as well.

You are strong enough to do this—you always have been. Athena's encouraging words landed in my heart, and I felt our bond pulsing with life and energy. She sent me a bolt of strength, almost implanting an image of my success in my mind. And that was all I needed to grasp hold of the venom.

And then I willed it to change.

Galvin screamed, an unearthly screech of pain as I evaporated the very essence of the vampire within him from the inside out. His scream echoed off the walls, sending the other vampires into an almost standstill as they covered their ears and watched as the corrupted heart and soul of the Nameless Hunters writhed in pain.

I felt something I could only describe as relief when the venom was gone, and his blood ran clear. My whole body felt weak, but the satisfied smile on my lips wouldn't fall away.

The screams subsided, and instead, he curled in on himself, panting. The vampires waited with bated breath. I felt Athena come up to me, tossing her arms around my throat, and instantly, the pain in my head dulled as Samara pressed a hand against my temple. Silas stopped near us, towing a pale and ashen Archer behind him and holding Jacob Bennett's body in his arms. I met their eyes gently, smirking.

Then I whispered words that changed everything. "He's mortal."

"No, no, no, no!" Galvin cried out.

An incredulous chuckle bubbled from my lips, and my coven followed suit, devolving into a disbelieving laugh. At the same time, the other vampires turned their malicious and hungry gazes back to the weak figure before them. They were more than prepared to take their lives back, to exact revenge for the years of torment and fear. They stalked toward him as he cowered.

But all I wanted was to leave this place and this chapter of our lives behind us. "Now's our chance," I said, glancing at my coven. Athena, Orpheus, Silas, Samara, and Archer nodded in agreement, their tired faces filled with relief, not a hunger for vengeance. We didn't need to finish him ourselves. We had done enough. This was their moment, their victory to claim.

"Let's go," I whispered.

We turned and made our way to the exit, our arms wrapped around each other. As we stepped out of the warehouse, I could hear the sounds of Galvin's desperate struggle behind us. The other vampires closed in on him, finally gifted their revenge. His screams were quickly swallowed by the sound of tearing flesh and snarling creatures.

We didn't look back. The night air was cool against our skin as we pushed through the doors, leaving Galvin to his fate. He had terrorized us for too long, but now he had faced the consequences of his hatred. The other vampires had seen to that.

For the first time in this second existence, I felt a sense of freedom. We had survived. We had won. And now, we could start to rebuild our lives, free from beneath the thumb of Nameless.

ATHENA

FIFTEEN

The three days following Doctor Kline Galvin's death were a whirlwind of emotions, tensions, and pain.

On the first day, we buried my father.

The sky wept as if mourning what could have been, the drops falling in a steady, mournful rhythm on our umbrellas. I stood at the grave's edge, the damp earth clinging to my boots, feeling a profound emptiness. I wasn't sad about losing him— I hadn't known him as a father, only as a distant, conflicted figure. What weighed heavily on my heart was the loss of what he could have been, the potential for redemption that would never be realized.

Archer stood beside me, his face a mask of grief and confusion. He was torn up, struggling with the complexity of his emotions. The man we were laying to rest had caused us so much pain, but he was still Archer's father. I felt his anguish like a physical weight, and my heart ached for my brother. He believed there could have been good in our father, even when all evidence pointed otherwise, and I think I was starting to believe it, too. I reached for his hand and held it in mine.

We had to bury him at night, as the sun was still my enemy— although I did have plans to rectify that very shortly. The moonlight was obscured by thick clouds, making the cemetery feel like an ethereal, almost otherworldly place. The rain soaked through our clothes, but none of us seemed to care. The Wanderers stood with me despite my insistence that they didn't have to. I knew my father had hurt them in ways more vicious than he ever harmed me. Yet here they were, a testament to the bond we shared and their unwavering support for me.

Orpheus, Silas, Laz, and Samara formed a protective circle around Archer and me. Their presence was a comforting reminder that we still had each other, even in the face of a loss this painful. Laz's hand found mine, their touch grounding me in the moment. Silas' stoic presence was a pillar of strength, while Samara's gentle caress on my back offered solace. Orpheus, ever watchful, scanned our surroundings, unable to shake the centuries of looking over his shoulder in only one day. I feared he'd be breaking his hard-learned habits and healing from his fear responses for a very long time.

The rain mingled with the tears on Archer's face, his grief pouring out silently. I wished I could take his pain away, but all I could do was stand by him, share the weight of his sorrow, and hope that time would eventually ease his heart. I let my mind send Archer a memory, the only good memory I have of our father. The moment he asked our forgiveness and when we granted him the chance to earn it.

My vision flashed gold as I sent the memory to Archer, and he squeezed back, choking on tears as he relived the moment with me.

A heavy silence fell over us as the final shovelful of earth was placed over the grave. I turned my head, seeing the distant silhouette of my mother's headstone. I couldn't bear to bury him beside her, but I think she'd want him to be near enough for me to visit if I ever wanted to. She was just selfless enough for that.

Archer knelt, placing a single pink rose on the freshly turned soil, his fingers lingering on the petals as if hoping to find some connection, some resolution. His shoulders shook with sobs. I knelt beside him, wrapping my arms around his trembling form. The ground was cold and wet beneath us, but that discomfort was far from my mind. All I could focus on was my brother's grief and the overwhelming need to comfort him. "I'm here, Archer," I whispered, my voice barely audible over the rain.

He nodded, his breath hitching as he tried to compose himself. "He could have been better," he choked out, his voice breaking. "He could have been so much more."

I hugged him tighter, the cold rain soaking us both. "I know," I said softly.

Together, we said goodbye to the father Archer mourned and the father I never had the chance to.

On the second day, Davia and Archer left to fulfill their promise.

The evening was heavy with the weight of goodbyes as I stood with Davia at the pier's edge, the salty breeze mingling with our whispered words. The waves lapped gently against the wooden posts below us, and I tried not to think of how many times it would crash between now and when Davia and Archer could return in one year's time. Davia's eyes glistened, her lips pressed into a determined line as she held back her emotions.

"What did you tell your parents?" I asked, eyeing the set of baby blue luggage at her side.

"Marketing Bootcamp," she replied flippantly. "They've been pushing me to leave the theme park for a while and branch out into bigger things." Her voice held an edge of regret. "Honestly, I found an online course I'm going to take while I'm there, so I'm not even lying."

"I hate that you have to do this," I whined, holding her hands in mine.

"Listen, as far as I'm concerned, it's a free vacation. And honestly, I would have promised even more years if it meant keeping you safe and alive." She squeezed my hands. Tears stung my eyes.

"I love you so much, Davia. You are my best friend," I vowed.

"Damn straight." She smiled. "I hope you realize that this better solidify my maid of honor spot in whatever weird quad blood-ritual wedding you're going to have. Okay?" She teased.

I chuckled. "You secured that spot the moment you told me you'd rock my world if you were into vagina," I smiled up at her. She pulled me into her, her arms tightening around me.

"Be careful, ok?" I whispered into her hair.

"Listen, I may have promised I'd be there for a year, but I didn't say shit about anything else. I'd like to see them try anything. Give me an excuse to use this new pepper spray I bought." She seemed confident, as always, but I noticed the slight twitch of fear cross her face. She was being brave for me. I hated it.

I nodded, my throat tight with emotion. "You're braver than anyone I know, Davia. But you don't have to be brave for me."

She sighed softly. Her smile dropped slightly as she gripped my face in her palms.

"I'm brave *because* of you, babe. You're kind of a badass survivor. You know that, right?" She pressed her forehead against mine, and together, we breathed, the rise and fall of our chests syncing. "You make me feel like I can be too."

She hugged me tightly, her warmth a brief solace against the chill of impending separation. "I'll be back before you know it. A year is like a second to you now," she pointed out before pulling back. "Besides, I have your backstabbing brother to keep me company."

I noted the look in her eyes. Outwardly, there was hatred, but I saw something else glimmering beneath the surface. I smirked. "Don't be too hard on him. I already forgave him."

"Yeah, yeah, well, I haven't made him suffer enough yet," she tossed before dragging me into one last hug. We held each other for a moment longer, and then she pulled away, her steps hesitant as she walked toward Archer, who was waiting nearby.

Archer's expression mirrored my own turmoil. His usually steadfast eyes were shadowed with grief. As Davia joined him, he took her bags and tossed them into the trunk of his rental car.

I walked over to my brother, my heart aching at the sight of him. We had been through so much together, and now we were being torn apart again.

"Archer," I began, my voice trembling. "I don't want you to go. I just found you. How am I supposed to say goodbye now?"

He looked at me, his gaze softening. "Athena, this isn't goodbye. You're the only family I have left. You're never getting rid of me." He chuckled and grunted as I threw my body at his.

I hugged him fiercely, feeling the familiar strength of his embrace. "Stay safe, Archer. Keep Davia safe. And come back to me."

He pulled back slightly, pressing a kiss to my hair. "You stay safe, too, Athena."

I nodded, blinking back tears. "I will."

"I love you, little brother," I admitted, and his answering tears were filled with relief and adoration.

"I love you too, sis," he confessed, playfully punching my arm.

"Don't go kidnapping anybody," I teased, and he rolled his eyes.

"I'm not making any more promises," he said, the double meaning obvious.

With one last lingering look, he released me and turned to enter the car. A hollow ache settled in my chest as I watched them disappear into the distance. The pier felt emptier, the world a little colder.

But I knew this promise had to be kept, a sacrifice they made to ensure our future. And though the goodbye was painful, at least they had each other.

Arriving at my little cottage, I tried to ignore how Archer and Davia's absence already had a pit growing in my stomach, but the void they left was too obvious.

I felt one of my mates press a kiss on the back of my neck and slip their arms around my waist from behind.

"They'll be ok, little nymph," Orpheus promised into my ear. "Elias is a bit of a jackass sometimes, but he's fair and honest. He won't harm them."

I nodded half-heartedly but bit my bottom lip.

"You don't believe me?"

"Silas' last promise begs to differ," I pointed out.

He gripped my arms, pinning them to my sides.

"Would I ever lie to you?" He asked, running his nose along the column of my throat. A shiver descended down my spine as I took in the hungry gazes of my other mates as they watched.

"No," I replied, breathily. My core tightened at his touch.

"Do you need a reminder of how devoted we are to you? Do you need us to show you why we'd never lie to you?" He asked tauntingly, letting his breath dust over my neck. I gasped sharply at the sensation.

The real answer. No, of course I didn't. These four showed me they loved me in every action. In every breath, in every movement. They remind me every day how lucky I am to have found them.

The answer I gave? "Yes, please."

I was such a liar.

A dirty, horny liar.

But I knew it would be worth it when Orpheus turned me in his arms to face him and devoured my lips in a punishing kiss. I sank into it, my arms, now free from his clutches, hung around his neck and pulled him to me. My hips pressed against his, desperately seeking friction.

His teeth bit my bottom lip, his fangs nipping at the skin there and flooding our mouths with the taste of my tangy blood. He moaned.

"Your taste haunts me, Athena," he licked my lip, drawing more of the blood into his mouth and sending a jolt of pleasure directly to my pussy. "It's all I can think about, all I can focus on."

He kissed me hard again, and this time, I dug my fingernails into his back. Groaning, he tangled his hands in my hair, holding me to him, unable to break free if I wanted to. I didn't want to.

"I need to taste more," he growled, and that was all the warning I got before he turned me around again and forced my torso forward, bending me at the waist so my face was pressed against the arm of the couch. I gasped as pleasure and shock mixed. My eyes caught Laz's, who was sitting on the sofa near my head, their hand gently stroking their length.

Orpheus hooked his fingers in my pants and pulled, taking my underwear with it and leaving me deliciously exposed to him. My ass was up, my face smushed into the material of the armrest, in such an undignified position I should have been self-conscious. But I couldn't think of anything but his tongue spearing into my cunt.

I cried out as he lapped up my arousal with eager swipes of his skilled tongue.

"Oh fuck," I cried out, gripping the back of the couch and bracing myself against his assault. Laz smiled at me with hooded, lust-filled eyes but made no move to touch me. Neither did Samara, who had come around to the back of the couch and looked down at me from her position, and Silas, who had kneeled next to the couch, a wicked smirk plastered on his face as much as I desperately sought their touches, I knew, like they seemed to know, that this was Orpheus' turn.

And boy, was he making the most of it.

His fingers dug into my thighs as he continued his relentless attack on my clit. My legs trembled, but he held me still. The pressure built in my core, a sensation I'd only experienced once before. His tongue worshipped my clit, and suddenly my arousal was squirting from me. Soaking his face. I cried out, weakly sinking my head and shoulders into the armrest as the aftershocks of my explosive orgasm wracked through me.

Orpheus hummed appreciatively, licking up every drop of my climax from his lips and my quivering pussy.

"That was the hottest thing I've ever seen, baby girl," Silas said, devilishly biting his lower lip.

I was too lost in the bliss of my orgasm to notice that Orpheus had stood and removed his pants. "Hold on to the couch," Orpheus commanded as he slammed his cock into me in one powerful stroke. I screamed out his name as he slammed into me over. Pistoning his hips like a starving man who could only find salvation within me.

My walls tightened around him, squeezing him, and he moaned. His breath was shaky and ragged as he neared his climax. He reached around, pressing his fingers against my clit as he fucked me.

I was a wanton little thing, crying out for more of his touch even as he pleasured me. He sped his hips and, therefore, his fingers, bringing himself to the edge of sanity and reason. He came with a roar, his cock pulsing inside of me and had me circling my hips, chasing after him to my own release.

We caught our breath, remaining still, just enjoying how our bodies were so in tune with each other. When he pulled back, removing himself from me, I opened my eyes and saw the feral looks in my other mates' gazes as they watched me.

"Our turn now," Silas said, pushing away Orpheus, who stepped back with a chuckle. I began to stand, but I felt Silas press a hand against the small of my back, keeping me bent over.

"I quite like this position," Silas mused, running his hands over my ass cheeks and down my legs, purposefully ignoring my soaked slit. "Let's put you to work, though, shall we?" He teased before gripping my hips and sliding up two feet to the left. The quick movement had me reaching out in front to brace myself. My hands braced against Laz's chest as we came to a stop with my head hovering just above their hard, aching cock.

I smirked up at them as they gently cupped my face. "What Silas is trying to say, in his caveman ways..." Laz kissed my lips softly. "Will you pleasure me with that perfect mouth of yours?" I moaned and nodded, my mouth falling open. Laz lifted their hips to relieve themselves of their pants, their cock sprung free, and I wasted no time circling the head with my tongue and sliding the whole thing into my mouth. Laz's head fell back, and they tangled their hands in my hair.

"That's my fucking good girl," Silas praised, and my whole body preened at the compliment.

"I'm going to fuck you now, baby girl." I shivered in anticipation. "Your job is to make our Laz cum before I do. Can you do that?" He asked, his fingers brushing against my swollen pussy lips. I sighed around Laz's dick and nodded.

A sharp slap came down on my ass cheek, and I jolted forward, my lips popping off Laz's cock in surprise.

"Use your words," Sials demanded darkly. I turned over my shoulder so I could meet his gaze. He was staring down at me like a man possessed. His eyes were hooded and eager, his breath coming in ragged spurts.

'Yes…sir," I replied, and then he was slamming into me. I fell forward, resting my head on Laz's chest as Silas fucked me hard.

"You're losing the race," Silas pointed out, and I suddenly remembered where I was. Stupid Silas and his mesmerizing dick. I dropped my mouth to Laz again and got to work. The sounds of their pleasure mixed together into a sinful cacophony, and I wanted nothing more than to keep eliciting those sounds for the rest of my life.

I took Laz as far down my throat as I could and then let my tongue dance along the tip as Silas pumped into me, hitting a part so deep that it had my body shaking with each punishing thrust.

Laz pumped their hips up, pressing their cock into my mouth, their abs tightening as they neared their climax. Silas, too, sped up, his thrusts becoming jerky and unstable as he prepared to fall over the edge of oblivion with me.

The three of us exploded into passion, one right after the other. I didn't know where my orgasm ended, and theirs began, but for several seconds, there was nothing but blinding passion.

Silas withdrew from my core just as I lifted my mouth from Laz's cock, licking my lips and smiling up at them.

Silas let go of his hold on my hips, and Laz helped me sink into the couch by their side. I hummed, satiated, and happy, loving the feel of their skin on my cheek. Silas knelt down, pressing their lips against Laz's, and I watched with rapt attention and a heart full of love as they found pleasure in each other. I felt delicate brushes of fingertips along my thighs and looked over my shoulder to see Samara. Her eyes were locked on mine and my skin felt heated under her chilled touch. She slid her fingers across the canvas of my skin delicately, not rushing, not expecting. Just relishing in the feel of my skin, and I leaned into her.

"I want you to touch me," I whispered to her, feeling as if we were the only two in the room but still feeling spurred forward by our audience.

She smirked, brushing her fingers across my pussy. She groaned at the wetness she found there. "You know we love you, right?" She asked, sliding her fingers along the slit again. I let my head fall against the couch as my legs fell open to give her more room.

I nodded in an almost lustful haze.

She circled my clit with one of her fingers gently, and my stomach tightened as the pleasure soaked through my limbs.

"You are everything we've always been looking for," she continued, pressing one finger into my heat. "I wanted love that didn't come at a price."

Laz smoothed their hand over my hair. "I wanted someone to see me for who I am, scars and all, and accept me anyway."

Silas sat near the edge of the couch on the ground, his eyes bearing into mine. "I wanted someone who would miss me if I left."

"And I.." Orpheus added from the armchair he'd taken residence on. "I wanted this. All of you. A family."

I felt tears sting my eyes, but the pleasure that Samara was gifting me chased the tears away.

I breathed deeply, loving the way Samara's fingers felt as they slid inside my slick channel. And then I let my mind drift to the first time I saw them. The way their bodies called to me, the way my heart instantly felt like it had been captured by the sinful strangers who saved me. I replayed the moment in my head and shared it. My vision blurred gold as I sent the memory to them as well. Their eyes flashed golden as they each joined me in that moment. The moment when it all began. The moment I fell for The Wanderers.

When the memory drifted away, and the golden hue dissipated, I felt the collective sigh of happiness and contentment. But it didn't last long before Samara's hands turned eager, and she slammed her fingers into me, bringing me to the brink once again.

She slammed her lips onto mine and kissed me like I was everything she needed. And I kissed her like I would never get enough.

When I came, soaking her fingers, she hummed happily before taking her fingers into her mouth and licking up my arousal.

I couldn't move, so instead of getting dressed, I simply pulled a blanket off the back of the couch and draped it over me. Laz and Samara cuddled into my side while Silas slid in next to my feet. Orpheus smiled at us from his spot across the room.

I felt their energies shift. An almost anxious cloud of worry blanketed the room. Orpheus and Laz shared a look.

"What's wrong?" I asked, pulling the blanket up to my chin. They didn't respond, but again, they shared a look. This time, Silas diverted his gaze and stared at the ground. I sat up, pulling the blanket tight against my chest.

"What's going on? What are you telling me?"

Laz cleared their throat. "We, um, well, we were talking about something, and we wanted to offer you something," they said timidly.

"Okay, what?" I asked, anxiety spiking.

"You know how we defeated Galvin?" They prompted.

"Yes…"

"We did something we never thought would ever be possible. We gave someone their human life back," Laz continued, looking down at their hands.

It all came into brutal clarity then.

They were offering me my humanity back.

My memories of my mother. My days in the sun. My small town for the rest of my days.

"Oh," I said, sorting through the mess of emotions that flooded through me.

"Is that something you want, bookworm?" Silas asked nervously.

Was it?

Did I want my old life back? I let the reality of what they were offering settle in my mind momentarily and tried to analyze my reaction to it.

"You're conflicted," Orpheus said.

My eyes flicked up to meet his. "I'm not," I answered.

"We won't be upset, Athena, if this is what you want," Samara added, squeezing my thigh.

"I don't."

They stared at me.

"I don't want to change this. This is my life. This existence, with you for the rest of eternity. This is who I was meant to be, and you are who I was meant to be with. This is my life, and I wouldn't change it for anything."

I heard their collective sighs of relief.

"Thank you for offering, but that version of me wasn't who I wanted to be. This is who I wanted to be. Thank you for giving me the chance to become her."

I met their smiles with my own.

"Ever since mom died, this place hadn't felt like home anymore," I whispered. "But right now, it does." I sighed. "I'll miss it."

"Why would you miss it?" Orpheus asked.

"Because we're going to be leaving?" I theorized. They were The Wanderers, after all. The very name implied nomadic tendencies.

"Athena, baby," Samara said, caressing my face. "This is your home, and for as long as it can be… It'll be ours, too."

"What?" I said, sitting straighter. "But you're The Wanderers, you wander," I emphasized.

"Darlin', we've been on the run pretty much from the moment we turned," Laz looked over at their coven. "I think I speak for everyone here that planting roots sounds perfect right about now."

I glanced around, finding the others nodding emphatically.

"We're going to stay here?"

"For as long as we can, Shockgrove is home," Orpheus confirmed, and I squealed in delight. I hadn't admitted aloud how much I would miss this place when we left. I knew that we couldn't stay forever. The neighbors would grow old one day, and we wouldn't, but that was long enough away that I didn't have to think about it now. All I cared about was that *this* was home, and *they* were home.

On the third day, I finally felt the sunshine again.

Zula, the New Orleans vampire with the gift of sun resistance, offered to perform her ritual on any other vampires who had assisted in the death of Galvin and Nameless. Fourteen vampires, including myself, met with her under cover of night at The Maine Plotline, and she gave us a chance at a sense of normalcy.

"Athena, is it?" she asked, her Cajun accent thick and warm.

"Yes, thank you, Zula, for coming to help us. Your numbers won this battle for us," I replied, gently clutching her hand.

"Not the battle, Ami." She patted my cheek, warmth radiating from her in waves despite the chill to her touch. "We just won the war."

I swallowed the lump in my throat and nodded, trying to fight back the tears that threatened to fall. Nameless had kidnapped me, tortured my mates, and killed Alora, but what they'd done to me and my mates was only a small portion of the hate and violence that they'd caused at the orders of Galvin. Nameless had been a black cloud of death and fear for vampires for centuries, and those vampires who survived them long enough have suffered greatly from their bigotry.

"How old are you?" I asked but quickly bit my tongue. "I'm sorry, you don't have to answer that! I was just wondering how long you've… yeah, sorry, never mind," I rambled.

She replied with a soft chuckle. "I have no way of knowing, for sure, but I'm pretty positive I am the oldest living vampire. So old that I remember a time before our King and Nameless."

I gasped.

"I've lived a long time, seen many things, and survived even more." She sighed. "I used to hide away in my compound. Afraid to step outside. But what kind of life is that? When your Orpheus sent us a message, I knew it was time for me to step out of the shadows. No matter how afraid I was. Or how much pain I harbored." She took a deep breath. "They took my mate," she said softly, eyes downturned. "Now, he rests peacefully for the first time."

I nodded my acknowledgment, knowing my emotions would betray me if I tried to speak.

"I met your Wanderers once before, a persistent bunch of fools," she teased. "They begged me to help them, to give them an advantage over Nameless. It wasn't till I saw the pain in their eyes and felt the sorrow in their souls that I knew they'd been hurt, as I have, by the Hunters."

She closed her eyes.

"They'd taken someone from them, too," she finished. "I recognized the broken pieces of their hearts because they looked like mine."

She turned her head toward the front of the store. Other vampires who had been freshly gifted the ability to walk in the sunlight were excitedly chatting with my mates, who seemed to enjoy the camaraderie of a community. Something else the Hunters had kept from them.

"They were barely living a half-life when I met them. Their wounds were fresh and raw. I think I gave in and performed the ritual just to give them something to live for. Our kind's numbers had dwindled too much to lose any more to broken hearts."

I let her words wash over me as I studied my mates' faces. How much pain have they suffered, and how long have they carried the weight of their trauma?

"Those vampires there," she indicated toward them, a slight smirk on her lips. "Those are vampires who have been made whole again. And I can see that they have you to thank for that."

I smiled. Watching my mates smile and laugh was like a balm against the burn of the scars on my heart.

"You've been around a while," I started. "Is it common to have multiple mates?"

"Well, no..and also maybe?" She must have seen the confusion on my face because she cleared her throat and continued. "There have not been many in our history. But it was not completely unheard of in incredibly powerful covens or with descendants of the royal family," she clarified. "But there's no way for us to know if it would have been more common had our kind not suffered a genocide of devastating proportions at the hands of Nameless." I nodded. "What is your vampire gift?" She asked.

"I can talk to my mates in my mind, from great distances too, it seems. And I think I can make people see what I want them to see, share memories," I added tentatively. "I haven't had much time to explore it, but I projected my memories into someone else's mind." I tried to ignore the sting of thinking about my father.

"Mental projection," she mused, nodding as if it made sense.

"You've heard of it?" I asked eagerly.

"I have," she replied cautiously. "The projectors I've met have something slightly different, but it sounds familiar. They have been able to establish an almost lethal grip on other's minds. Able to bend them and shape them as they desire. I bet if you needed to, you could too."

I shook my head.

"I hope I never need to," I replied, not enjoying the feeling in the pit of my stomach.

"We agree on that." She rubbed her chin. "The projectors I've met each had suffered something unimaginable. Something that made them feel so alone that their souls called out to the fates for someone to connect to. Someone to understand. Someone who can see and feel what they do." She nodded when she saw the recognition on my face.

"If I had to guess," she started, smiling at me. "I'd say it's not your gift that ties you together, but the experiences that gave you your gift in the first place."

"You're telling me that because I suffered, because I went through unimaginable pain, the fates or whatever wanted to reward me with multiple mates so I wasn't lonely?"

"I'm telling you that what you survived yesterday is what gives you your strength today." she clarified, gripping my hand in hers. "Trying to understand fate is like trying to bottle a feeling. Useless. And a waste of the moment."

I nodded. Enjoying the way that thought made me feel.

"Are you ready to walk in the sunlight again, Athena?" Zula asked, her smile warm and comforting. I nodded.

"Yes, yes, I am."

The ritual was quick, but the pain was vicious. She helped me lay down on the couch at the back of the Maine Plotline and whispered words over my body while her hands dusted touches along my skin. It started as a low hum of energy in my bones, a vibration almost like I was sitting in a massage chair. It wasn't painful at first, but it was slowly growing more aggressive. The pinpricks of pain grew into stabbing shooting jolts as the power seeped into my blood. It was agony. The fire seemed to course through my veins, igniting every nerve ending. I clenched my fists, nails digging into my palms, trying to anchor myself through the pain. My muscles began to tremble uncontrollably, the spasms wracking my body. It felt like I was being torn apart and remade, every cell of my body rebelling against the intrusion.

My vision blurred with tears, and I could barely make out Zula's form through the haze of pain. She placed her hands on my shoulders, and I could feel her power surging into me, a force both ancient and overwhelming. The heat intensified, morphing into a searing sting that felt as if molten lava were being poured into my veins. My skin felt too tight, as if it would split open at any moment.

I couldn't contain it any longer. A guttural scream tore from my throat, the sound raw and primal. The fire inside me roared, consuming everything in its path. Every nerve was alight with excruciating pain, each breath a struggle against the searing heat.

"It's almost over," Zula murmured, her voice cutting through the torment.

I forced my mind to drift to Laz, Samara, Silas, and Orpheus. Their faces, their love, their unwavering support. It gave me something to hold onto, a lifeline in the sea of agony. The burning began to ease, replaced by a deep, pulsing ache that resonated through my entire body.

I opened my eyes, and the world came back into focus. The pain was still there, but it was a dull throb compared to the searing agony of before. I felt...different. A new energy coursed through me, a resilience that hadn't been there before.

Zula helped me to my feet, her grip firm and steady. I saw my mates had come to surround me, their faces a mixture of pain and sadness. They did not want to see me in pain.

"I told you that you didn't have to be here for this," I whispered, my throat still feeling raw from the cries.

Silas hugged me first, but Laz and Samara quickly joined in. I chuckled, feeling the pressure of their bodies on all sides.

"Get in here," Silas grunted toward Orpheus.

"I thought I told you I don't share," he joked, a teasing heat in his eyes. Silas reached his hand out, gripped the front of Orpheus' button down, and pulled him into the embrace. We devolved into a fit of relieved laughter. I caught Zula's eyes as she nodded, smiling before turning and leaving us.

I held tightly to them. My mates. My heart. My happy ending.

I could live forever and still never get enough of them. I guess it's a good thing I had an eternity.

ACKNOWLEDGMENTS

How have we already reached the end of this story? I cannot thank you all enough for joining me in this world and falling in love with Athena and her Wanderers the same way I have. There are countless people who deserve to be thanked for their support in making this series a reality.

First, to my husband for being my first Beta reader and biggest cheerleader. Thank you for always being there to hype me up.

Then, my mother. You not only taught me how to tell a good story, but your support is the reason I get to do this. So thank you.

To you, dear readers, for spending the last two years in Shockgrove, Maine, with me. I can't express just how much your love and support has meant to me. I see all your messages and your posts, and every time I see you all tell me how much you love this world and these characters, I feel like maybe I'm doing something right. Thank you for it all.